Darkness in the Sky

The noises and actions of battle continued to swirl around him. A young officer on a white horse nearly ran over him. Guns, men, and horses all headed toward a gap in a nearby fence. Officers shouted orders, and the soldiers cursed and wailed. Henry, his head still spinning, saw the first hints of darkness in the sky.

As Henry stumbled away from the activity around him, the guns roared in the distance. They belched smoke and howled angrily, like demons guarding a gate.

READ ALL THE BOOKS
IN THE wishbone classics SERIES:

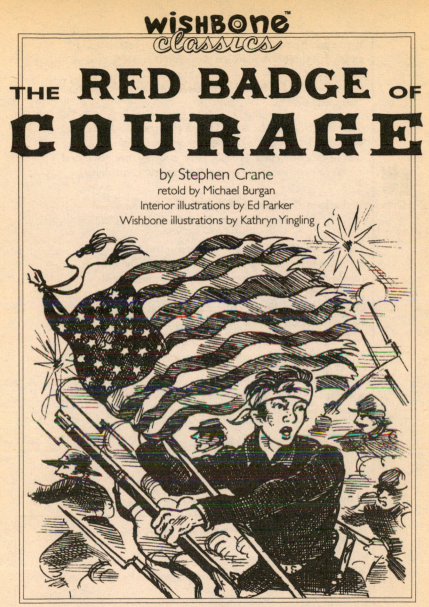

WISHBONE™ CLASSICS

THE **RED BADGE** OF **COURAGE**

by Stephen Crane
retold by Michael Burgan
Interior illustrations by Ed Parker
Wishbone illustrations by Kathryn Yingling

HarperPaperbacks

A Division of HarperCollins*Publishers*

This is a work of fiction. The characters, incidents, and dialogues are products of the author's imagination and are not to be construed as real. Any resemblance to actual events or persons, living or dead, is entirely coincidental.

HarperPaperbacks *A Division of* HarperCollins*Publishers*
10 East 53rd Street, New York, N.Y. 10022

Cover photographs by Carol Kaelson

A Creative Media Applications Production
Art Direction by Fabia Wargin Design

First printing: December, 1996

Printed in the United States of America

HarperPaperbacks and colophon are trademarks of HarperCollins*Publishers*
WISHBONE is a trademark and service mark of Big Feats! Entertainment

❖ 10 9 8 7 6 5 4 3 2

HENRY FLEMING

Introduction

All set to enter a world of action, adventure, drama, and laughs? Then come along with me, Wishbone. You may have seen me on my TV show. Often I am the main character and sometimes I am the sidekick, but I'm always right in the middle of a thrilling story. Now, I'm going to be your guide as we explore one of the world's greatest books — THE RED BADGE OF COURAGE. Together we'll meet a lot of interesting characters and discover places we've never been! I guarantee lots of surprises too! So find a nice comfy chair, and get ready to read with Wishbone.

Table of Contents

Stephen Crane

Let me introduce you to Stephen Crane, the author of THE RED BADGE OF COURAGE. As you read you might think that Crane had spent years in the army and that he had lived in the muddy trenches on a battlefield. Crane did see fighting firsthand—but not until after he wrote his masterpiece! Crane's great imagination helped him write the colorful descriptions in THE RED BADGE OF COURAGE.

Stephen Crane was born on November 1, 1871, in Newark, New Jersey. He was the youngest of fourteen children. His father, a minister, died when Stephen was eight. Mrs. Crane, a journalist, struggled to raise her family by herself. Stephen was often sick as a child, and illnesses would haunt him later in life. But he was high-spirited and enjoyed such sports as football, baseball, and boxing.

When Stephen was sixteen, he helped his brother Townley run a news agency. Here, he started his writing career as a journalist, tracking down local news stories. The next year, 1888, Crane entered college. He attended three different schools but never graduated.

After leaving his third school, Crane went to New York City and started working there as a journalist. He also wrote for small papers in New Jersey. But Crane's writing was often too fancy—instead of just giving the facts, he wanted to explore how and why things happened. Crane was a creative writer at heart, not a journalist.

In 1892 Crane published his first short stories. They featured the colorful descriptions of people and places he would use in his novels. The following year, he finished his first major book, *Maggie: A Girl of the Streets*. He also started *The Red Badge of Courage*, finishing it in 1894. Crane was just twenty-three years old.

Almost immediately, Crane won great praise for his account of the inner struggles of the book's young hero, Henry Fleming. Critics also said Crane described the sights and sounds of battle very realistically, just as if he'd been there himself. One Civil War veteran even claimed that he remembered fighting with Crane at a major battle. Crane, however, was born six years after the war ended! Like any good writer, Crane took what he heard and read about the war, then used his imagination to bring it to life.

Crane always tried to experiment with his writing. He was called one of the first modern American writers. He disliked the sentimental books popular in his day; he wanted instead to describe life as it really was, good and bad.

Two years after publishing *The Red Badge of Courage*, Crane finally got the chance to see war for himself. He became a war correspondent, or journalist. He traveled to Greece and wrote about a war there. He also went to Cuba and Puerto Rico to cover the Spanish-American War of 1898. (He volunteered to fight in that war, but the U.S. Navy rejected him.)

While in Cuba, Crane marched beside American soldiers as enemy gunfire whistled overhead. Sadly, while he was there, he also caught malaria, a deadly disease. Crane died on June 5, 1900. He was just twenty-eight years old.

Many people have wondered what other great books this powerful author might have written if he hadn't died so young. But Crane's skill and intelligence remain to this day, in *The Red Badge of Courage*.

THE RED BADGE OF COURAGE is Stephen Crane's best-known work. In his day, it made him famous around the world. Today, this story of one young man's growth during a Civil War battle continues to be widely read by American students.

Stephen Crane first wrote *The Red Badge of Courage* as a short story. Then he turned it into a novel, or longer story, and published it one section at a time in newspapers. Finally, in 1895 Crane published the complete novel as a book, and within a few months critics in America and England were praising him and his work.

Always trying to find the right word or phrase, Crane wrote many different versions of the book—at least seven. Some modern versions of *The Red Badge of Courage* include parts that weren't published while Crane was alive. After writing his first draft, Crane talked to soldiers who had fought in the Civil War to get more details about the sights and sounds of battle. He also based the book on tales he had heard from his teachers in college about the war.

Crane believed war was dehumanizing—that is, it took away a person's identity, almost turned him into a nameless body. To make that point, Crane gave only some of the characters names. Even Henry Fleming, the hero, is called simply "the youth" for much of the original book.

At first, Crane called the book *Private Fleming: His Various Battles*. Henry Fleming not only battles the enemy but also his own fears. Later, Crane crossed out that title and wrote beneath it the more colorful title we know today: *The Red Badge of Courage*.

The Red Badge of Courage has been called a psychological book. That means it focuses on Henry's deepest thoughts and feelings. We learn about Henry and his struggles by reading about what happens inside his head.

Although Crane never fought in a war before he wrote the book, he said his background in sports helped him write it. "I believe," he wrote, "that I got my sense of the rage of conflict on the football field." *The Red Badge of Courage* was one of the first popular books to show both the horrors and bravery of the Civil War in a realistic way.

MAIN CHARACTERS AND SETTING

Henry Fleming — a teenager from New York who fights for the North in the Civil War

Jim Conklin — Henry's friend from his hometown

Wilson — a soldier Henry meets when he goes to battle

The lieutenant (Hasbrouck) — a young officer in Henry's regiment

The tattered soldier — a wounded man Henry meets after a battle

The colonel (MacChesnay) — one of the commanding officers in Henry's regiment

Military Ranks

The characters in *The Red Badge of Courage* hold different ranks in the Union army. This list shows the order of ranks, from highest to lowest. Henry Fleming is a private, the lowest rank in the army. Henry and his fellow soldiers are part of a *regiment*, a group of about five hundred to one thousand troops.

General

Lieutenant General

Major General

Brigadier General

Colonel

Major

Captain

Lieutenant

Sergeant

Corporal

Private

The two armies in the Civil War went by several names:

NORTH	SOUTH
Yanks	Rebs
Yankees	Rebels
Union/Federal	Confederate
Blue	Gray

Setting and Time Period

*T*he Red Badge of Courage takes place during the American Civil War. This terrible war that divided the United States began in 1861 after the Southern states left the United States to form their own country, the Confederate States of America. For many years, leaders from the Northern states and the Southern states had argued about slavery. Many Northern states wanted to stop the spread of slavery into new states and territories; some wanted to get rid of slavery completely. Most Southern states depended upon slavery for their economy. When Abraham Lincoln, who was opposed to slavery, was elected president in 1860, the Southern states began to secede from, or leave, the United States.

Stephen Crane's book *The Red Badge of Courage* takes place in a Southern state during this war. Some military experts say that the battle Crane describes is based on the Battle of Chancellorsville, which took place in Virginia. That battle was fought in early May 1863. The South, led by Generals Robert E. Lee and Stonewall Jackson, outfought the North, which was led by General Joseph Hooker.

The Civil War ripped America apart. Friends and

families often fought on opposite sides, and more than a half-million soldiers died. The war ended in 1865, when the Southern general Robert E. Lee surrendered at Appomattox. The Southern states rejoined the Union, and the freed slaves received their first legal rights. President Lincoln is still admired today for preserving the splintered nation while upholding the promise of the Declaration of Independence: "All men are created equal."

1
Rumors of Battle

Whew! Am I tired!

Sometimes things don't turn out to be the way you thought they would. Take me, for example. Sometimes I imagine myself to be an army dog—a brave and heroic  **soldier, just like Henry Fleming wants to be in THE RED BADGE OF COURAGE. So I take off early in the mornings on long marches through the woods. Then I get lost! Not to mention tired, sore, dirty, and hungry. Army life isn't at all what I imagined it would be.**

Sometimes you can't tell how you're going to face a challenge—like marching off to war. You want to do your best, but reality may be different from your dreams. Sometimes your fears sneak up on you. And sometimes you surprise yourself and find courage you didn't even know you had.

Henry Fleming learns all about being afraid—and being brave. He's a boy not much older than you. Henry volunteers to join the army during the Civil War. The war takes place in the 1860s and pits the Northern states against the Southern states. Henry wants to help the

North defeat the South—and to fight courageously in battle. You'll read all about Henry's dreams and the reality he finds as he struggles with his fears. Get ready for Chapter 1 of THE RED BADGE OF COURAGE!

The morning chill and fog melted away as the sun rose above the hills. All along the riverbank, the soldiers, in their brown huts, awakened and stirred in the camp. Across the winding black river, the distant fires of the enemy were out.

This morning, the soldiers buzzed, passing the words down the line. A tall private had heard the rumor from someone down by the stream. They were finally going to fight.

Who are these soldiers? They're Northern troops in the Civil War. They were also called "Union" or "Federal" troops. The Southern troops across the river are the enemy. They are also called "Confederates" or "Rebels"—"Rebs" for short. Each side is also sometimes known by the color of the uniforms—blue for the North and gray for the South.

Henry Fleming watched the tall private run excitedly from one group of men to another. He pulled thoughtfully on the brass buttons of his blue uniform. Still just a boy, Henry had brown hair and eyes—eyes that looked deeply at every new thing he saw. Everything he saw in the army was new to him.

The tall private waved his arms as he spoke, saying the rumor had to be true—he had heard it from a friend, who heard it from a friend, who had a brother near the battle. Henry inched closer, trying to hear what the soldier said.

"It's gotta be," the private said to the men around him. His name was Jim Conklin, and his blue uniform hung like a worn rag from his thin body. His arms and legs stuck out far beyond his pants and shirt.

"It don't gotta be true at all," another soldier said.

"We're going up by the river," Jim insisted. "We'll cut across, then sneak up behind the Rebs."

The soldiers turned to each other in small groups and argued about Jim's message. Some swore it had to be true this time. Others kicked the ground in disgust, calling it a lie.

"How many times have we heard that before?" a soldier named Wilson questioned loudly. He spat on the ground as he eyed Jim Conklin. "Eight times in the last two weeks," Wilson said, answering his own question. "And we haven't moved yet. We're not gonna move today, or tomorrow neither. Those generals and majors in charge don't know a hill of beans about fighting."

Some of the men nodded, agreeing with Wilson. "They'd have us sit here and rot," Wilson continued, "without blinking an eye."

Wilson's loud voice made him seem bigger and older than he was. But he was just a youth like the other soldiers gathered around. Wilson rubbed his smooth cheeks, then pushed his red hair out of his eyes.

"It's true, I tell ya," Jim Conklin said again. He drew closer to Wilson. "Are you calling me a liar?"

"Maybe I am," Wilson said with a sneer.

The soldiers raised their voices, some agreeing with Jim, the rest with Wilson. **Hmm, it seems that if the Northern troops don't move soon, their first battle might be in their own camp.**

Henry sat and listened to the heated debate. He and the men had heard so many rumors about fighting. Each time, Henry's heart had pounded as he thought about firing his gun or bravely charging through the enemy's bullets. After a while, Henry left his fellow soldiers and crawled into the little wooden hut he now called home. He needed to be alone, to think about what he had heard.

The hut had wooden crates for chairs, and the walls were logs loosely stacked together. Rifles hung from posts nailed into the walls. At the far end of the room, a fire burned weakly. Some of its smoke missed the chimney and circled back into the room. Henry sat down and stared out the one tiny window.

So we're going to fight at last, he said to himself.

Henry wasn't sure why, but he believed Jim and his rumor of a battle. Henry had dreamed of this moment for so long. At home, lying on his bed, he had stared at the ceiling and imagined wars from the past. As if he were staring at a brightly colored painting, he could see images of heroic men thrusting swords and firing cannons. Those men, he knew, had fought bravely.

In his imagination, Henry had heard the clash of metal on metal, smelled the trampled earth and blazing battle fires, and felt the rush of galloping horses and running troops. He had always wanted to have the same kind of adventure, to win glory for his acts of courage. Now, if Jim Conklin was right, he would have the chance to make his dreams of being a hero come true. He would soon know the excitement of battle.

Henry thought back to the time before he joined the army. **Do you know what a "flashback" is? Sometimes, in a book or movie, characters think about what happened in the past. You get to find out what happened at that time. Henry is flashing back to the time before he left his home to go to battle.**

Before Henry left the farm, his mother tried to discourage him from enlisting. She didn't see the glory of war, the way Henry did. In the village, he heard the townspeople gossip about the battles down South and the young men who had already gone to fight. The newspaper told of great Union victories. All these words of war mixed with Henry's daydreams of battle. The images stirred something in his heart—he had to fight.

"Ma," he told his mother, "I want to enlist. I want to fight for the North."

"Henry, don't you be a fool," she said, and turned away from him. That ended the discussion.

The next morning, Henry enlisted anyway. He returned home wearing his uniform proudly. His eyes beamed with delight. He hoped that his mother would feel differently when she saw him. Henry wanted her to share his pride and joy.

But Mrs. Fleming didn't praise him, and she didn't try to stop him. She simply said, "The Lord's will be done." She knew nothing would stop the boy from following his dream.

Sadly, she helped him get ready, even knitting socks for him to take. When it was finally time for him to leave, she packed his bag, putting in the socks and all his best shirts.

"If you get a hole in your clothes," Mrs. Fleming said, "you be sure to mail 'em home so I can fix them. And I'm giving you a jar of blackberry jam. I know it's your favorite."

Mrs. Fleming stopped her packing for a moment. She looked up to give Henry some advice:

"You take good care of yourself, Henry, you hear? Just remember you ain't the only soldier out there. There's no need to be a hero. Follow your orders, and watch yourself. You're just a boy in the middle of all those men. Watch yourself."

"Yes, Mama," Henry said.

"And remember," Mrs. Fleming went on, "if it comes time to shoot your gun or face being shot, you do what's right. Don't think about me. Just do what you have to do. Here, take your things. Be a good boy."

"Yes, Mama," Henry said.

That was all she said. It seemed odd to him. He had expected a grand speech from his mother about his bravery. He had imagined he'd say something powerful in return, almost poetic, like the speeches he had read in the great books about war heroes. Instead, her cheeks stained with tears, Mrs. Fleming just handed him his bag. Henry took his things and headed off to war.

On the way to the train station, Henry stopped at the school to say good-bye to his friends. The students eagerly gathered around him and the other boys who had signed up to fight.

"Lookit those uniforms," one girl teased. "Why, Henry, don't you look the brave soldier."

Henry ignored her. Instead, he studied a brown-haired girl. She looked sadly at him, then turned her gaze away. As he left the school Henry looked back over his shoulder and saw the girl at the window, watching him. She turned away again as Henry's eyes caught hers. He wondered if she might worry about him as he fought the Rebs. Later, he often thought about her and that moment.

Henry set off for Washington, D.C., and all along the way people cheered him and the other brave young soldiers. *This is more like it*, Henry thought. The cheers made him proud to be a soldier fighting for his country. He had done the right thing. The war would be glorious, and he would do many brave things. But after he got to the training camp, Henry learned that a soldier's life wasn't as grand as he had imagined.

Henry thought he would be fighting right away. Instead, his regiment spent months at the training camp. Even when the troops reached the battlefield, they sat there like a bored dog on a summer's afternoon. The troops practiced marching and fighting, then sat. Practiced some more, then sat some more. To pass the time, Henry twiddled his thumbs or tried to imagine what real war was like.

Once, when Henry was on guard duty, he looked across the river that cut through the camp and saw a Rebel soldier, also standing guard.

That's my enemy, Henry said to himself.

They talked for awhile.

"Hey, Yank," the Reb called. **"Yank" is short for "Yankee." That's a nickname for a Northerner.**

"Whattaya want?" Henry replied slowly.

"Yank, you're a darn good fella."

Henry felt regret. For a moment, he was sorry he had come here to fight—and maybe to kill.

But all those thoughts and feelings were in the past. Now, lying on his back,

The flashback is over—Henry is back in the present, lying down in his little hut.

Henry thought about the battle to come. One question

filled his head. It repeated over and over, like a drumbeat: Would he run?

He closed his eyes and imagined himself surrounded by blazing guns and slashing bayonets. He remembered stories he had heard about the Rebs— how they fought so fiercely, and how they marched into battle, like machines that couldn't be stopped.

"No, stop!" Henry shouted, jumping to his feet. "What's the matter with me?"

The question in his head took him by surprise. Henry felt like a little boy again, just learning about the world—and about himself: Who was he? Was he a fighter? Or was he a coward?

The sounds of voices shook Henry from his thoughts.

"It don't matter, I tell ya," Jim Conklin said, entering the hut. "Don't believe me. But if you just sit here and wait, you're gonna see I was right."

"Oh, because you know everything," Wilson said, following him in.

"Never said that," Jim replied. He turned away from Wilson and started packing his knapsack.

Henry cleared his throat. "Are you sure, Jim? We're gonna fight?"

Jim didn't look up from his task. "Sure enough. Just wait till tomorrow. There'll be the biggest battle you ever saw."

"I don't know, Jim," Henry said cautiously. "We've heard those stories before."

"Didn't the cavalry leave this morning? Something's happening this time, I tell ya." **A "cavalry" is a group of soldiers who fight on horseback.**

Henry let the words sink in. Finally, he spoke.

"Jim?"

"What?"

"How do you think the regiment will do?"

"They'll be fine, once they start fighting. I know we're a bunch of fresh fish, but there's plenty of old-timers out there too. We'll all be fine." **"Fresh fish" is Civil War slang for new soldiers who have never fought.**

"Do you think . . . do you think any of those boys will run?" Henry asked with hesitation.

"There's always some who run. It's only natural when the bullets start flying for the first time."

"Here he goes again," Wilson said impatiently. "The soldier who knows everything."

"I didn't say—" Jim began, but Henry interrupted him.

"Jim! Do you think you'd run?" Henry tried to laugh, as if he were just joking. Wilson laughed a bit too.

"You know, Henry, sometimes I see myself up there with my gun in my hand, and if everyone around me was running, I'd probably run too. But if everyone stood there together, why, I'd stand and fight. You can bet on it."

Henry liked Jim's answer. He saw that everyone had some fear, some uncertainty. Henry felt better now.

2
Henry's Big Question

Although Stephen Crane invented the character of Henry Fleming, there were many young men like Henry during the Civil War. Millions of soldiers— Northern and Southern, black and white—fought in the war. Some, like Henry, volunteered. Maybe, like Henry, they thought war would be full of glory.

When Henry awoke the next morning, he heard the news: Jim was wrong. The regiment wasn't going into battle. Some of the soldiers teased Jim and made fun of those who had believed him. One even picked a fight with him.

The men returned to their usual activities—sitting and waiting. Now Henry had even more time to worry about how he would act on the battlefield. He began comparing himself with the other soldiers. He had known Jim back in his hometown. Jim had said he'd stand and fight.

Well, Henry said to himself, *I'm just like Jim. I guess I'll fight too.*

But what if Jim were wrong? Henry started talking to other soldiers, trying to see if they shared his doubts. He'd feel better knowing he wasn't the only one who thought about running, who worried about his courage. But Henry never came right out and said what he was really thinking. He kept his deepest thoughts to himself.

Just as the men yesterday had argued about Jim's rumor of a battle, Henry had his own debate going on in his mind.

They're all heroes, he sometimes thought. *These fellows around me, they'll fight to the death.*

No, no, he thought at other times, *they're just like me. They don't know what they'll do. Everyone has the same fear. How can anyone know what he'll do before he does it? Any man who brags about how brave he is—well, he's a liar.*

Henry felt bad about having these thoughts. He had no right to think poorly of the other soldiers. Henry wished he didn't have so much time to think. Why were the generals so slow to get them into battle? He blamed them for this delay. Why couldn't they just give the order to fight? Henry imagined the generals sitting in their own camp high above the river. They didn't seem to care that the soldiers had to wait so long.

Henry's anger at the generals began to boil up inside him, like the thick, black coffee the men heated over their campfires. Henry stomped around the camp, cursing under his breath like an old veteran. **A "veteran" is someone who has experience doing something. A veteran soldier has already been in a battle, unlike a "fresh fish" such as Henry.**

The waiting dragged on for days. One morning Henry heard the men again whispering rumors of battle. In the eastern sky, Henry saw a yellow patch, the first glow of morning. The patch was like a welcome mat laid out for the rising sun. Then, a black shadow cut across his view. It was the colonel, riding a huge brown horse. Behind the colonel, the red fires of the Confederates burned like the fiery eyes of a dragon. A dragon, Henry thought, that waited to devour him and his comrades.

A corporal rode up to the colonel. Was this it? Henry wondered. Was this the order to march? After a moment, the corporal rode away.

"Don't forget the box of cigars!" the colonel called out after him.

Cigars? Henry said to himself in disbelief. *We're all sitting here itching to fight, and he's worried about his cigars?*

But within a few minutes, the colonel did give an order to march, and the men began to move. The soldiers stirred slowly, grabbing their guns and slinging their sacks over their shoulders. Henry imagined looking down on the troops from a mountaintop—from a bird's-eye view. Moving along the hill, the men must have looked like a long black serpent emerging from a hole. The rumble and creaking of the rolling cannons filled Henry's ears. At last, they were finally on the march!

As they tramped along the muddy paths some of the men still couldn't agree whether they were really going to battle.

"You see?" Jim Conklin said. "You wouldn't listen to me. We're gonna fight this time, I know it."

"Conklin," Wilson said, marching behind him, "you don't know nothing for sure but your name, and sometimes I think you get that wrong."

Once again, the men were split in their opinions. Henry didn't join in; he was still having his own personal debate.

Slowly, the human serpent formed by the marching soldiers slithered from hill to hill. As they moved along Henry heard the older soldiers talk happily of fighting again. Even the new recruits stepped lightly, as if they were heading to a Saturday dance, not to the battlefield.

"I feel kinda sorry for them Rebs," one soldier said. "Pretty soon, they ain't gonna be tasting anything but Northern bullets."

Henry felt separate from all this. His doubts were like a wall, cutting him off from the other men. Some of them laughed and joked or even pulled pranks. One fat soldier sneaked away as they passed a farm and stole a horse grazing near the gate. The soldier smiled broadly as he walked off with his prize.

"Hey, Yank!" a young girl cried angrily from the house. She bolted out the door and chased the soldier. She grabbed the horse's mane and pushed the soldier away. The rest of the regiment stopped to watch and laughed at this small battle.

"Go get him, miss!" one soldier shouted.

"Hit him with a stick," another man advised, slapping his sides as he laughed.

The men cheered wildly as the girl won the struggle for the horse. They teased the solider as he returned to the regiment. Henry paid no attention to this excitement. He just marched along silently, still deep in his own thoughts.

As night began its slow slide down the hills the troops stopped and set up their tents. Henry remained off by himself. He walked away from the men, looking back now and then. The campfires danced eerily, and Henry felt a shiver as he watched their strange red lights flickering against the purple evening sky. He lay down in the grass and closed his eyes. A soft wind stroked his face. The darkness and quiet felt comforting—it matched his sad mood.

Henry imagined himself back home on the farm. He saw himself doing his chores. He could feel the old gray cow—the spotted one—next to him as he milked her. The image stirred a pleasing warmth in his stomach.

"Maybe I ain't cut out to be a soldier," he mumbled to himself, breaking the dark silence. "I ain't like the others here. How'd I ever think I could fight?"

"You talking to yourself, boy?" a voice asked with a laugh.

"Wilson?" Henry questioned the darkness.

"What are you doing out here?" Wilson asked, now coming into view.

"Just thinking."

Wilson took out his pipe and lit it.

"You're getting kinda blue, ain't ya? What's got you so down?"

"Nothing," Henry said weakly.

Wilson puffed on his pipe, sending clouds of smoke around his head. "Boy, I tell you, we got them Rebs right where we want them. We're gonna lick 'em good!"

"I thought I heard you complaining about all this marching today," Henry said coolly.

"The marching ain't so bad," Wilson replied, "if it leads to some fighting. What I can't stand is those generals moving us here, moving us there, then making us sit for days."

"Jim says we'll probably see plenty of fighting," Henry said.

"I hate to say it, but your friend may be right for once. It's gonna be a big one, I can tell. And we're gonna beat 'em!"

Wilson stood up, excited by his own confident words. He paced in front of Henry like a caged animal who knows its cage door is about to open.

"You're going to do great things, I suppose." Henry was surprised to hear the bitterness in his own voice, but Wilson didn't notice the harsh tone.

"Oh, I don't know," Wilson said simply. He was trying to be modest. "As well as the rest. I'll hold my own. Least, I'm gonna try."

"How do you know you won't run?"

"Run?" Wilson laughed. "Run? 'Course I won't run."

"But how do you *know*?" Henry persisted. "Lots of good fellas say they'll fight. Maybe they even dream about being a hero. But when the time comes, they run like rabbits into the woods."

"I suppose it happens to some like that," Wilson said. "But don't you bet on my running. You'd lose a bundle."

"You talk like you're the bravest man in the world."

Wilson grew angry. "I ain't never said I was the bravest man in the world, or even this regiment. All I said was I'll do my share of fighting. Who do you think you are, Henry Fleming, talking to me like that?" Wilson quickly turned his back on Henry and stormed back to camp.

"Well, you don't have to get so mad about it!" Henry called out. Wilson ignored him.

Henry sat alone again in the darkness. He'd hoped Wilson would say he was scared—that he, too, worried about running. Henry had to know that Wilson and the others were just like him. But Wilson was ready to fight and maybe to die. The others were too. Henry felt different from everyone else—and so alone.

He returned slowly to his tent and stretched out on a blanket. Jim's snores carried through the damp air. As Henry lay in the darkness he saw himself in battle. He imagined a monstrous beast calling in his ear.

"Run, Henry!" the beast cried above the gunfire and shouts of battle. "Run for your life!"

In this dreamlike vision, only Henry heard the beast. The other soldiers fought on, deaf to its words. The image made Henry sweat, and his stomach tightened. Finally, exhausted from his worry, Henry drifted off to sleep.

Henry's got some pretty strong doubts about how he'll act when it's time to fight. Can Henry overcome his doubts? Will he fight when the time comes? Keep reading to find out!

3
On the March

Even with the war all around them, Henry and the other soldiers are wondering if they'll ever see a real battle. The next day, they move out again and march through the fields.

The soldiers marched all day and crossed two bridges as another night began to creep over them. The reflections of a fire twisted and jumped on the water. Henry studied the fields all around him. The buzz of insects filled his ears as the men set up their camp.

It could come at any minute, Henry thought to himself. *The Rebs could attack in waves, and the regiment would be doomed.* He looked through the darkness, trying to see if any uniformed shapes were crawling through the dusk's shadows. Nothing stirred. Henry lay down and quickly fell asleep, tired from the day's march.

In the morning, Henry had very little time to check out his new surroundings before the regiment began moving again. Day after day, Henry and his comrades repeated the same actions: march, camp, sleep. As this went on, the soldiers began to toss off equipment and clothing they didn't need, trying to lighten their loads. They no longer felt like fresh fish, even if they hadn't fired their guns at the enemy. But the real veterans, the soldiers who knew the smell of gunpowder and the cries of dying men, still laughed at the inexperienced troops.

Days passed, and then one gray dawn, Henry awoke with a start.

"Get up, Henry," Jim said, nudging him.

"What is it?" Henry asked, still clearing a dream from his head.

"Don't know. But everyone's moving fast. Let's go!"

Henry quickly packed up his things and slung his rifle over his shoulder. It bounced against him as he ran. He heard the soldiers talking as he rushed by them.

"Why're we in such a rush?"

"What's going on?"

"Know anything new?"

Henry also heard a noise ahead, like the rat-a-tat of a drum. Gunfire. He tried to think and run at the same time, afraid that if he stumbled, the others would trample him into the dirt. He looked around and saw other regiments pouring out of the woods.

This is it, Henry said to himself. *I'm finally gonna see whether I run or fight.*

But at that moment, Henry couldn't have run away even if he wanted to. He was surrounded on all sides by soldiers—a human fence that penned him in.

"Why'd I come here?" Henry muttered, panic rising in his throat. "I didn't want to enlist. They made me—the government, everyone. And now I'm gonna be killed like a pig at harvest time!"

> **Henry has forgotten—or has chosen to forget—that he volunteered to fight.**

The men ran down a bank and crossed a stream. Thousands of them, like swarming ants, moved up a hill, a mass of blue moving against the green grass. Henry heard the boom of cannons up ahead. When they reached the top, Henry looked out and saw lines of blue and gray firing at each other. This was just a skirmish. **A "skirmish" is a small battle, with just a few soldiers, fought usually before a major battle.** Watching soldiers dart among the trees fascinated Henry. The Union troops formed a dark path that cut across a field gleaming orange from the sun. A Union flag fluttered in the morning breeze, its red stripes bold against the blue sky.

Running with the others, Henry tried to notice everything around him. He saw a body lying up ahead. A dead soldier! The first he had seen. The dead soldier lay on his back staring at the sky. A gray toe stuck out of a hole in the man's worn boot. The other soldiers in the regiment steered clear of the body, but Henry looked deeply at the man's pale, chalky face and red beard. The wind moved the whiskers, as if a hand were stroking them.

Henry was drawn to the dead man. He wanted to examine the body closely. Henry wondered what would happen if he stared into the dead man's wide, lifeless eyes. Would he find any answers to his many questions?

The men marched on past the skirmish. The landscape seemed to grow dark. Everything began to look evil, threatening. A coldness ran through Henry's body. Huge shadows loomed everywhere.

What if the Rebs are out there? Henry wondered to himself. *They could be waiting for us to run right into them.*

Henry suddenly lost faith in the generals. They were all stupid, he thought. The regiment was rushing into a trap. He wanted to warn the others, tell them to stop. He looked at the faces around him. No one else seemed to share his worry. They were ready for war.

Henry still wanted to shout a warning, but he knew the other soldiers would make fun of him. Suddenly, the regiment came to a halt. The men talked quietly about the battle to come. Some built little walls of branches and rocks. They hoped these walls would protect them from Southern bullets. But before they could get settled, the order came to fall back, to return the way they had come.

"That way?" Henry demanded, pointing in the direction from which they had come. "Why did they march us out here in the first place?"

Jim Conklin just shrugged, and the men returned to their old position.

"I can't take this much longer," Henry went on.

"Yeah, my legs are killing me," Jim said.

But Henry wasn't thinking about his legs. He was thinking about finding out if he would have courage to fight or if he would run away. He had to throw himself into battle to find out. A battle would change him, Henry thought. He would be a better person for fighting—if he fought.

After covering old ground most of the morning, the men started in a new direction. Henry's fears ran wild again.

Maybe it's just better to die, he said to himself. *Just get it over with and end all this doubt.*

What was death? Henry wondered. Like sleep, he guessed. But without any nightmares that made you soak yourself with sweat. And no more waking up to face your fears. With death, there would be no more doubts.

Cannon fire interrupted Henry's thoughts. He saw more soldiers ahead of him, and the hot, dangerous flashes of their rifles. The noise of the battle grew until it sounded like a train roaring toward him.

"Henry."

Henry turned. Wilson stood beside him. His face was white and his lip trembled.

"Henry," Wilson repeated heavily. " I think this is it for me. I'm gonna die today, I can just feel it."

Wilson reached into his pack and took out an envelope. His whole body shook. He thrust the package into Henry's face.

"Here, take this. It . . . it's for my folks. If something happens to me out there, you make sure they get it, Henry, okay?"

"Wilson, what are you—?"

Wilson raised his hand, signaling Henry to say nothing. Wilson looked lifeless, like he was already lying in his grave. He let his arm drop, then silently turned away.

4
The Battle Begins

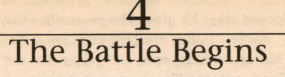

It looks as if Wilson isn't feeling as brave as he was a little while ago. With the first battle about to begin, Henry isn't the only one who has doubts.

Henry saw men running through the haze that clung to the battlefield. His regiment waited for orders and passed along rumors of the fighting.

"The general says he expects us to see the worst fighting of the whole war."

"I hear our boys are getting it bad over on the left. Them Rebs pushed 'em right back into a swamp."

"A fella from Maine, he says they'd been fighting for five hours and they musta killed thousands of Rebs. One more battle like that, he says, and the war will be as good as done."

The talking died down as the sounds of battle drew closer. An artillery shell screamed as it soared above them, then exploded in a red cloud of fire. Henry felt pine needles rain down on him from the blast. Bullets whistled overhead, ripping through branches and tearing at trees. Twigs and leaves sailed down to the ground. **"Artillery" is another name for cannons and other big guns. The ammunition they fire is called "shells." During the Civil War, some shells were solid, like cannonballs; some had gunpowder and bullets inside and exploded like the one that just whizzed by Henry.**

Up ahead, Henry saw their lieutenant take a bullet in the hand. The young lieutenant swore, holding his injured hand away from his body to keep the blood off his uniform. In the distance, a battle flag waved in the wind, barely rising above the smoke. Men dashed through the haze, running away from the battle, and the soldiers in Henry's regiment raced about wildly, like a mob pushing first one way and then another. The veteran regiments hooted and hollered insults. Their voices joined with the shrieks and whistle of bullets to create a grim song of battle.

All around, officers on horseback galloped wildly, shouting at the fleeing men. In the middle of this confusion, Henry knew he would run, too, if his brain could get control of his legs, but the noise and the sights glued him in place. As he watched soldiers retreating from the main battle ahead Henry realized he still had not seen the enemy. He imagined the enemy was a monster, like a fire-breathing dragon. He had to see it, at least once, even if he did run away after.

"Here they come!" someone shouted.

The soldiers loaded their rifles. Henry saw Jim tie

a red handkerchief around his neck, then wait patiently with his loaded gun.

"Here they come!" the cry rose again.

Henry squeezed the rifle in his hands. This was it, he thought—his first battle was about to begin. One moment he pictured himself fighting bravely, ignoring the roar of the guns and the blinding gray smoke. The next instant Henry imagined himself throwing down his rifle and turning in fear. Even with the battle so close, he still didn't know what he would do.

A gray swarm of yelling men burst through the fields choked with smoke. Henry panicked—had he loaded his rifle? He couldn't remember. And he had no time to check.

Behind him, a general screamed at his regiment's colonel. "You've got to hold 'em back," he shouted. "You've got to!"

"Yes sir, General," the colonel replied as confidently as he could. "We'll do our best."

The general rode off. The colonel fiercely repeated the general's order, trying to stir his men.

"We're in for it now," a soldier near Henry mumbled. "We're in for it now."

"Don't shoot till I tell you to," a captain shouted as he walked among the men. "Wait for my orders, you hear?"

Henry felt sweat pour down his forehead and cheeks, and pool above his lip. Without thinking, he aimed his rifle and fired a wild shot. He froze—had the

43

captain seen him disobey the order not to fire? But the captain wasn't in sight, and Henry quickly reloaded. His worry and doubts from before seemed to have dried up like a puddle in the hot southern sun. **The guns the soldiers used only fired one bullet at a time. Most rifles were reloaded by putting a bullet and gunpowder down the barrel, then tapping it down with a metal rod.**

Henry felt the presence of the men around him. They weren't strangers—they were brothers. And they all had the same goal. He was not just Henry Fleming, farm boy. He was part of a team, one piece in a well-made machine. He and the other men had a job to do. Their regiment, army, and country were in danger, and they had to protect them.

Inside his head and his heart, Henry's old fears turned into a red rage. He felt like a trapped animal ready to defend itself against a pack of wild dogs. He wanted to strangle the enemy with his bare hands. As he realized how little he, just one soldier, could really do, Henry's anger burned even stronger.

All around, the Union soldiers waited for the order to fire. When it came, their rifles went off like fireworks crackling on the Fourth of July. Henry kept shooting and reloading, not even thinking about what he was doing. He struggled to breathe as the foul-smelling smoke clung to the ground. He heard voices all around him, but they sounded far away, as if he were half asleep. He heard more clearly the sounds of soldiers reloading their guns and firing into the smoky cloud in front of them. The battle filled Henry's senses and made him dizzy.

Out of the corner of his eye, Henry saw the wounded lieutenant standing with a man who had run screaming when the first shots flew. The soldier wailed like a baby and stared, sheeplike, at the lieutenant. The officer grabbed the man's shirt and slapped his face. The blows drove the soldier back toward the troops. The soldier tried to reload his gun, but his hands shook so much that the lieutenant had to do it for him.

Henry knew that some of the men had already been shot. Some were slumped over, dead. One soldier near him was grazed in the face. Blood flowed from the wound. The soldier put his hands in the red stream and ran from the battlefield. Another man took a shot in the stomach. He grunted, then fell backward to the ground. A third soldier screamed as a bullet shattered his kneecap. Crying for help, he wrapped his arms around a tree to keep himself from falling.

The sound of gunfire slowly changed from a constant roar to occasional pops. At last, Henry saw the Rebs scattering into small groups and running off. The Northern troops yelled with relief. They whooped and whistled over their victory. Some of the soldiers silently slumped against trees, too exhausted to celebrate. Henry felt the heat of rage that had carried him through the battle drain from his body. He noticed how dirty he was, with grime plastered to his hands. His throat ached from the smoke. He took a long swig of warm water from his canteen.

"We held 'em back!" a few men called to each other, slapping backs and shaking hands. "We did it!"

Henry looked around and felt strangely calm. There were dead bodies twisted in odd positions— arms bent at crazy angles and heads turned in strange directions. It was as if some giant had opened a bag above them and let the bodies fall to the ground.

Groups of wounded men shuffled off to the rear. On nearby hills, the fighting still raged. Cannons seemed to be talking to each other—a blast of loud questions followed by a booming response. A nearby cannon fired, and Henry jumped. He imagined the gun was pointing right at him.

Henry thought nature did not seem to realize a battle had just taken place. The sky was a deep blue, and the sun cast a golden light on the green trees and fields. And yet, in the middle of all this beauty, men shattered nature's quiet with explosions and stained the earth with death.

But it was over, Henry thought, and that was the important thing. When a Union soldier carrying a flag went by, Henry felt a warm rush of pride. No man had ever fought as bravely as he. He smiled to himself, satisfied. He heard the men still congratulating each other.

"Let's hope we don't see any more fighting for a week," one man called out, and the soldiers around him laughed in agreement. But before the laughter could fade, an amazed shout rose above it.

"Here they come again! The Rebs are coming again!"

Henry looked up. He saw the Rebels charging. In front, a soldier dressed in gray held the Confederate flag. He seemed to be rushing right toward Henry.

5
Wild Dash

Shells fell like huge raindrops, and Henry watched them explode in the woods. The Confederate soldier continued racing toward Henry. A Union shell burst near the Reb and sent him tumbling to the ground. More Rebs streamed forward. The Union soldiers grumbled as they reached for their rifles again. They seemed to move in slow motion, while in the field the Rebs kept charging toward them.

"We need more men!" someone shouted, his voice shaking. "How do they expect us to fight the whole Rebel army by ourselves?"

Other men nodded, again cursing the generals who ran the war.

"Pipe down!" the young lieutenant ordered as he darted among the troops. "Keep your mind on the Rebs."

Henry saw waves of gray uniforms coming toward him. *It can't be*, he thought. *We're not really going to fight again. We've done our job.* But the bullets began ripping through the trees once more. Smoke quickly covered the field. The haze looked yellow in the sunlight and blue in the shadows. Henry saw the enemy's flag rise above the smoke and move forward.

Henry's body began to shake. His knees felt weak, and his muscles burned with pain. More of the men began to shout in fear, demanding that more troops be sent. But for now, Henry's regiment was alone, and he wondered if extra men would get there in time. Henry imagined the Rebels as supermen. They were stronger than the Union troops—faster, braver. Where did the Rebs find the strength to charge again? They were more like machines built from steel than like men.

Trying to load his rifle, Henry found he had no strength in his arms. He stood there, looking out through the smoke and watching the enemy advance. He waited, frozen, like a mouse waiting to be gobbled by a menacing cat.

A soldier next to Henry suddenly threw down his gun and howled in fright. He ran off into the woods. Another man, who a moment ago had looked so brave, now turned pale. He, too, threw aside his rifle and fled. One or two other soldiers followed their example, dropping their guns and dashing away through the smoke. It seemed to Henry as though everyone around him was running from the battle.

Menacing cat? Where?

"Ahhh!" Henry screamed. Fear rose up from the deepest part of his gut. He spun around and lost his sense of direction. He staggered around like a chicken with its head cut off. No matter which way he turned, he knew he faced death.

Finally, he found the strength to move his legs. He turned his back on the fighting and ran as if he were being chased. Henry ran faster and faster, away from the shots and shouts of battle. He dropped his rifle, but he didn't care. His cap flew off in the woods, but he didn't think for a second about stopping to pick it up. He ran for his life.

The look of horror covered Henry's face. Anyone who saw him would know that fear filled every inch of his body. He sprinted past the lieutenant.

"All you men!" the officer cried. "Get back to the lines! Hold your ground! Cowards!"

The lieutenant madly swung his sword, but Henry did not slow down. Once or twice, he stumbled and fell, then quickly picked himself up and continued his wild dash into the woods. Henry didn't feel much safer as he moved farther from the fight; even the sounds of battle seemed dangerous.

Other soldiers raced ahead of him, and Henry could hear more coming up behind. It seemed to him that the whole regiment was fleeing. Henry ran faster, thinking he had to stay ahead of the men who trailed him. If the Rebels came after them, they would shoot the men at the rear. Henry did not want to be one of them.

Shells screamed over his head. One exploded in Henry's path, and he fell to the ground. He sprang up again, unhurt, and zigzagged off in another direction, cutting through some bushes. He came to a Union cannon blasting into the distance. The soldiers loaded and fired over and over.

"You poor fools!" Henry tried to yell. "The Rebs are coming! Save yourselves!"

But the soldiers didn't hear his weak cries. A rider galloped up to the cannon, and Henry saw the young man's face. He shook his head.

This is a fella, he said to himself, *who will soon be dead.*

Running up a small hill, Henry stopped for a moment and looked back. He saw a brigade moving up to the front line. **A "brigade" is a group of regiments.** Would it be destroyed too? Henry moved on, slowing to a walk as the sounds of battle faded behind him. He saw a general sitting on his horse. Other officers rode up to the general, then took off again.

The general frowned as he received information about the fighting. Henry inched closer, trying to hear what was being said. He wanted to describe to the general the horrors he had seen and to tell him to order a retreat. Any fool could see that the men were going to die. Maybe the general didn't understand how badly the battle was going. Henry could tell the general all he needed to know.

The general didn't give the order to retreat. Henry felt anger stir inside him. He wanted to jump on the general, pound him with his fists and swear at him. Didn't the general see that he had to do something? He had to save the men in the field. Henry stayed close by, hoping for the chance to tell the general what he knew about the battle.

"Tompkins!" the general barked. "Tell Taylor to halt his brigade and take a regiment over to the woods. Tell him to hurry!"

A soldier saluted as he took the order and rode toward the battlefield. A moment later, another messenger rode up at full speed, his horse kicking up a cloud of dust. The young soldier jumped off his horse and ran to the general. Henry couldn't hear the soldier's words, but he saw a small smile slip across the general's face.

"By heavens, they have?" the general shouted gleefully. "They stopped 'em in the woods! They stopped the Rebs!" He turned, smiling, to the men around him.

"We'll wallop 'em now," the general said. "We'll wallop 'em!"

Henry watched the general bounce excitedly in his saddle. The officers around him shared his happiness as they repeated the good news.

Henry slumped against a tree, realizing what had happened. His regiment hadn't been swallowed alive. Somehow they had held off the Rebel attack. Conklin and Wilson and so many others had fought hard and won. Henry rested his head on his knees. He could hear cheering coming from the battlefield.

Boy. Henry's probably not feeling too good about himself right now. I wonder what he is thinking?

6
Into the Woods

Henry wanted to be a hero, but he forgot one important thing. He's just a boy! He ran from the fighting because he was scared, and now he's trying to convince himself that running away was the right thing to do.

Henry looked out toward the fighting. From the shouts he heard, he knew the Union troops were advancing against the enemy. He turned away, amazed. Anger bubbled up inside him again.

I did the right thing by running, he told himself. *I was going to be killed for sure. Wasn't it my duty to stay alive so I could fight again when we could win? But them fellas who stayed . . . what were they thinking of?*

Henry felt he had been the smart one; the soldiers who stayed were just too dumb. But those dumb ones had somehow found a way to win! If they'd been smart, they would have known it was impossible to hold the line. But somehow they did the impossible. Henry felt as if his fellow soldiers had let him down. They had made him look bad.

"Fools!" Henry spit out. He'd have to listen to the men curse and tease him if he ever made it back to camp. But Henry knew he was right. He had been the smart one. Henry felt a wave of self-pity wash over him, and he cursed the war and the men on both sides who fought it. **Henry is making excuses for running. Sometimes people make excuses to convince themselves they did the right thing—even if inside they know they did something wrong.**

Henry walked along, his emotions churning inside. He crossed the field into the woods. Henry had to get far away from the sounds of shooting in the distance. The crackling shots were like voices that taunted him for running. He went deeper into the woods, past prickers and vines and young trees. The noises of war finally grew more faint.

These woods are so peaceful, Henry thought. Here, the war seemed like a nightmare he had dreamed long ago. He playfully tossed a pinecone at a squirrel. The animal ran off, chattering. It stopped on a nearby branch and trembled as it looked down at Henry.

Henry was just like that squirrel or any other animal. When danger looms in front of you, you run. He didn't have to feel ashamed for what he had done.

Henry left the squirrel and walked deeper into the woods. He brushed against branches, and the noise covered up the faint booms of the distant cannons. Ahead of him, a grove of trees bent and twisted together. It formed what looked like a tiny chapel.

Henry paused outside this chapel, then entered. Dried pine needles covered the ground, making a soft, brown carpet. Henry felt at peace in this place, almost as if he had stepped into a real church on a Sunday morning. But he gasped and drew back when he saw what was staring at him.

Two eyes peered at him, wide and empty. A dead man sat propped against a tree. The soldier's blue uniform was now faded green. The eyes bore through Henry like cold steel spikes. The man's dull expression reminded Henry of a dead fish. The mouth drooped open and its once-red lips and tongue were now yellow. Tiny black ants marched across the soldier's gray skin. One group of ants was carrying something over the man's lip.

"Aaahhh!" Henry heard his shriek pierce the forest's quiet. His scream sounded as if it came from far away, not from his own mouth. His body froze, and he couldn't stop gazing into those empty eyes. He took one small step backward, then another. He crept away, not daring to turn his back. Henry feared that if he looked away, the dead man would rise up and chase him.

He backed into a branch. It pushed against him, and his feet tangled in a vine. He almost fell toward the dead man. He shuddered at the thought of touching the cold, stiff body.

At last, he broke free and ran. In his mind he could picture the black ants crawling toward the soldier's dead eyes. The thought made him run faster. After a time, he stopped, panting heavily. He imagined a strange voice would come from the dead man's throat and call after him. But all Henry heard was a soft breeze through the trees. Even the insects had quieted.

Then, suddenly, a huge blast ripped into the silence.

7
Death of a Friend

As the battle rages on, Henry is about to come out of the woods. He's now a deserter, a soldier who has left the battle without permission. What will happen when he rejoins the troops?

Henry ran toward the sound of the fighting. It was strange, he realized, that he was running toward something he had just escaped. But a hidden excitement pulled Henry forward to watch the battle.

Henry realized that the sounds of the forest had stopped. The forest was silent, as if listening to the noises of the battle being fought nearby. The rifle screams and cannon roars were louder than the battle Henry had fled. As Henry ran through the woods, branches and vines kept tripping him and slowing him down. It was as if the forest didn't want him to leave and face death. But Henry kept moving, circling around the thickest trees and bushes.

The cannon blasts grew louder. Henry kept going forward, looking for the easiest path. As he walked he imagined the whole war as a machine, a gigantic and terrible thing that did one job very well—kill men.

He understood now that he and his comrades had been foolish. They had imagined their little skirmish would settle the whole war. In truth, the regiment was just a tiny part of the war, a blade of grass in a huge field.

Henry saw more dead soldiers as he walked along, their bodies baking in the midday sun. He tried to push their images out of his mind. Coming to the edge of the woods, Henry finally reached a road. Alone, he continued down the road and watched wounded Union troops, their blue uniforms stained with blood, dragging themselves down the lane, away from the fighting. The men cursed their injuries and walked in pain.

Henry overheard a soldier complain to another, "If that general knew the first thing about keeping his men organized, this thing wouldn't be dead." The soldier tried to lift his wounded arm, which hung limp at his side.

Another injured soldier sang to himself, changing the words of a song Henry knew: "Sing a song of victory, a pocketful of bullets, five and twenty dead men baked in a pie."

Some of the men stumbled along like zombies, the walking dead, their faces gray masks. One of them was a tall battered soldier who looked ready to drop dead at any second.

Henry watched as two privates carried an officer.

"Be careful, Johnson, you fool," the officer commanded. "Don't shake me so much! Do you think my leg is made of iron? Hey you, soldier," the officer now gestured to a wounded man in the road. "Out of the way. Let me through, let me through."

The wounded soldier cursed the officer as he went past.

Henry walked alongside the men, studying their wounds. He fell in next to a tattered soldier. The man's uniform was blue shreds, and his skin was covered with dirt. Blood and gunpowder stained his clothes. He was listening to a sergeant nearby telling tales of war. The tattered soldier's mouth was open in amazement.

"Careful, boy," the sergeant said to him with a smile. "You'll be catching flies if you keep your mouth open much longer."

The tattered soldier pulled back, embarrassed. Henry saw that he had two wounds—one in his head, the other in his arm. The arm dangled like a broken tree branch ready to snap off.

"Was a pretty good fight, wasn't it?" The tattered man directed the question at Henry.

"What?" Henry had been deep in thought. Now he looked more closely at the soldier with the dirt-caked face and lamblike eyes.

"Pretty good fight, eh?"

"Y-yes." Henry tried to walk a little faster. The man kept pace.

"I never imagined men could fight like that," the tattered soldier continued. "But I knew the boys weren't no cowards, neither. Just give 'em a chance, I always thought, and they'll show you what they can do."

He looked to Henry for a response. Henry was silent. The tattered man began again.

"I heard a fella from Georgia one night. He was standing guard duty and making fun of us. 'You Yanks will run when the first bullet flies,' he said. 'No sir, mister,' I said, 'our boys will fight like men.' And we did. We fought and fought and fought."

The man's face was filled with pride as he talked about the army he loved so much. He cleared his throat and looked closely at Henry.

"Where you hurt, boy?"

Henry froze. Panic inched up his body.

"What?"

"Where you hurt?" the tattered soldier repeated.

"Why, I, I mean, well, uh—"

Henry turned quickly and blended into the crowd. His face burned with embarrassment. The tattered man, confused, looked at him in astonishment. Henry kept moving farther back, away from his questioner. Henry now felt he wore his shame like a coat, for everyone to see. It covered his body. Could everyone tell he was a deserter? Did they know he had run away?

Henry looked at the wounded men around him. Why couldn't he be like them? Why couldn't he have a bloody wound, his own red badge of courage?

Aha! I bet you wondered what that meant. To Henry, a wound is a sign of a soldier's bravery.

Henry found himself next to a gray-skinned soldier. Other soldiers whispered about this wounded man and offered advice. The man motioned for them to go away, to leave him alone. With each step the gray soldier's body stiffened. His lips seemed to be holding back a deep moan of despair. Something in the way he moved drew Henry's attention.

"My gosh!" Henry yelled. "Jim Conklin!"

Remember Jim? He's Henry's old buddy from home.

The tall gray soldier smiled a little. "Hello, Henry."

"Oh, Jim! Oh, Jim!" Henry saw fresh red blood ooze over the dried black scabs on Jim's wounds.

"Where've you been, Henry?" Jim asked flatly. "It was quite a battle today, wasn't it? Yes sir, quite a battle."

"Oh, Jim!" It was all Henry could say, seeing his friend in such bad shape.

"It was a circus, let me tell you. And I got shot! How about that. I got shot."

Henry reached out to support Jim, but the wounded man pulled away. Then, suddenly, Jim drew closer. His voice was a shaky whisper.

"I'll tell you what I'm afraid of, Henry. I'm afraid I'll fall down here in the road and some wagon will ride right over me. That's what scares me no end."

"I'll take care of you, Jim!" Henry blurted. "Don't worry about a thing. I'll watch out for you."

"You sure, Henry? You'll do that for me?"

"Sure, I'm sure," Henry asserted. "I'll take care of you."

Jim continued to beg Henry. "I was always a good friend to you, wasn't I, Henry? I've always been good to everybody. I'm not asking too much from you, am I? I . . . I'd do it for you—you know that, Henry."

"I know you would, Jim," Henry said. He could hardly speak as he gulped back his sobs.

Suddenly, Jim turned away. He stood straight again and ignored Henry's attempts to help him. Jim seemed to be deep in thought, maybe wondering what would happen when death finally came.

"You'd better get him out of the road, son," a voice said. Henry turned and saw the tattered soldier. He had dragged himself alongside Henry. "Them wagons come down this road like a house afire, and your friend could be run over in a second." He lowered his voice. "The poor devil's a goner anyway. You can see that, can't you? Five or so minutes, and he's dead."

Henry took the man's advice and tried to lead Jim to the field by the side of the road.

"C'mon, Jim, come with me," Henry said. "You'll be safer over to the side."

"Huh?" Jim responded slowly. "Oh. The field?"

Henry looked up the road as he started to reach for Jim's shoulder. A wagon was heading right for them! Just as Henry turned back to Jim he heard the tattered soldier scream:

"He's running!" the tattered soldier gasped. "Catch him!"

Jim was stumbling and staggering away from them into a clump of bushes by the road. Henry and the tattered soldier ran after him. They caught him easily.

"Jim, Jim, what are you doing?" Henry asked.

"No, don't touch me, don't touch me," Jim begged. "Leave me be."

Jim stumbled forward again. Henry and the tattered man stayed near him, but not too near. It was as if they were afraid to get too close to him, afraid Jim might turn on them. At last, Jim stopped. His face looked contented, as if he had found the exact spot he was seeking. Jim stood very still, then his chest began to heave. His body shook, as if a wild animal trapped inside was kicking and clawing to get out.

Henry's face twisted as he felt his friend's agony. He sank to the ground and sobbed.

"Jim, Jim!"

Jim waved his hand. "Don't touch me . . . leave . . . me . . . be."

A shiver rippled through Jim's legs, making them do a hideous dance. His arms beat wildly, like a crazed

Helllooo! Start flipping the book pages and check out the action . . . . Woo-cha!

bird unable to fly. His body stretched up to its full height, then slowly fell to the ground. It bounced a bit as it hit the earth.

"Good Lord!" the tattered man cried.

Henry watched, unable to look away. He finally sprang to his feet and moved closer. Jim's mouth was open and his face was frozen in a strange laugh. The wind blew open his jacket, and Henry saw his red, bloody body. It looked as if he had been chewed by wolves.

Henry stood up, raging. He shook his fist at the battlefield. The war—that bloodthirsty monster, that perfectly oiled killing machine—had destroyed his friend.

8
What Now?

Back on the farm, it was easy for Henry to imagine himself a war hero, covered in glory. But the reality is more like a nightmare. And the war has now cost him a good friend.

Henry's stomach twisted into knots as he thought about what he had just seen. Jim's horrible death left him feeling weak.

The tattered soldier stood with his hands on his hips as he shook his head.

"Now, wasn't that something?" he said. The man didn't seem bothered at all by Jim's death. "I never seen anything like that before. He was a strong one, gotta say that. Wasn't that something?"

Henry wanted to block out the man's words with a scream of grief. He threw himself on the ground. The tattered man stood above him for a moment.

"Lookit here, friend," he finally said. "Your friend's dead, and that's too bad, but we're still here, and we gotta take care of ourselves. He's fine here, let's leave him be. Let's worry about us. I ain't doing so great myself, you know."

67

Henry looked up at the tattered man. "You, you ain't gonna—"

"No, I ain't gonna die. But I could use some rest. Some rest," he said dreamily, "and a nice big bowl of pea soup."

The two of them said nothing as they headed back to the road, back to the parade of wounded men. Finally, the tattered soldier broke the silence.

"I'm not feeling so good anymore right now. Yup, I'm starting to feel pretty darn bad."

"Good Lord!" Henry said, afraid to watch another painful death.

"No, no, it ain't that bad. And if I do die, it won't be like what that fella did. That was the strangest thing. Me, I'd just flop over wherever I was. You know, I didn't even know I was shot at first. Fella standing next to me told me so. I started to pull back, and another bullet caught me, nearly spun me around. Hey, you ain't starting to look so good yourself. Where did you say you got hit? I've seen fellas get shot and not even know it, but let me tell you, I felt that second one, yes sir."

The man looked closely at Henry again. "So where did you get hit?"

Henry had been squirming ever since the soldier started talking about wounds. Now he waved his hand in disgust.

"Oh, don't bother me," Henry said. He could have strangled the man, he was so angry. Everything the soldier said added to Henry's shame. "Don't bother me," Henry repeated.

"Well, 'scuse me," the tattered man replied. "Lord knows I don't want to bother nobody."

Henry's anger and guilt swirled together. His mind raced; he didn't know what to do. Why did the man pester him like this? Henry didn't want to leave the tattered man alone and helpless. But he couldn't bear to talk about what he had done during the battle. He didn't want to think about it anymore. Finally, Henry made up his mind.

"Good-bye," Henry said suddenly, and took off across the field.

"Hey! Where you going?" the man demanded. "Now, don't run off."

Henry climbed a fence and kept walking. He stumbled around the field, not knowing where to go or what to do. He was a deserter. He had run like a coward instead of fighting like a soldier. The tattered soldier's questions had felt like knives jabbing at his heart. Henry knew there would be others asking questions. How long could he avoid answering them?

Henry wandered back to the road. More wagons and men cluttered it now. The soldiers seemed to be retreating. So Henry wasn't alone leaving the battlefield. Perhaps, then, he wasn't so bad after all. But soon he noticed other troops moving forward, toward the fighting.

"Outta the way," these soldiers called, pushing

strongly through the crowd. They seemed eager to fight. Their faces were proud and serious, and the officers rode tall, with stiff backs, on their horses. Henry felt his sadness return. These new men were so sure of themselves, as if they knew they were specially chosen to do good things. They were like the war heroes Henry had read about in his books, the men who first inspired him to go to war. He had dreamed of being a hero too. But he had shattered those dreams. He could never be like these men. Why had he thought he could? Henry almost wept.

He felt so many things. First it was sadness and guilt. Now envy filled his heart. He wanted the same strength these soldiers around him had, the same courage. He wanted to change places with one of these heroic men and try again to make his youthful dreams come true.

He imagined himself fighting bravely, a blue warrior leading a charge. If he died, he would die bravely too. The picture made Henry feel better. It was good to know he could still imagine himself doing brave deeds. Just because he ran once didn't mean he was a coward forever.

Henry suddenly laughed to himself —he was so jumbled up inside! Was this what it was like to grow up and be an adult? He could cry one minute, then picture himself a hero the next. The mixture of emotions left him weak inside.

With all the worries and fears running through

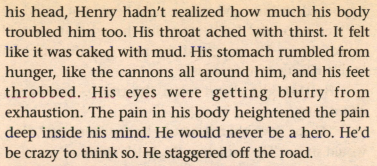

his head, Henry hadn't realized how much his body troubled him too. His throat ached with thirst. It felt like it was caked with mud. His stomach rumbled from hunger, like the cannons all around him, and his feet throbbed. His eyes were getting blurry from exhaustion. The pain in his body heightened the pain deep inside his mind. He would never be a hero. He'd be crazy to think so. He staggered off the road.

But in the middle of all this agony and confusion, Henry had one clear thought: he should return to the front. He stopped and looked at himself—how could he return like this? He had no rifle. And how could he ever find his regiment? But he could get a rifle easily enough. And he could fight with any regiment. He debated in his mind what to do. How, Henry wondered, could he explain his absence? Why was he returning unhurt? His burning desire to return began to die out.

But Henry couldn't stray too far from the sounds of the battle. Like a moth to a flame, Henry kept heading back toward the fighting. He had to know who was winning. He wanted to know that the Union troops had done well, even though a loss would make him look better. In a battle when things turn bad and your side is losing, regiments scatter, men run off in all directions. It would be harder for others to label Henry a coward if his side lost.

Henry tried to think of a tale to tell his regiment if he ever made it back—something that explained what happened to him and where he'd been. But could he lie well enough? Each story he thought of seemed weak, phony. He imagined the men questioning him and laughing at his excuses.

He thought about what the troops would say about him.

"There goes that deserter, Henry Fleming," they would sneer. "He ran when the battle started."

"You don't say?"

"A no-good coward, eh?"

Henry could picture the men pointing as he walked by, and he saw himself stuttering as he tried to explain what he had done. But his words would never silence the troops' taunts. They would insult him whenever they saw him, or tell jokes about him behind his back. And when the next battle came, all eyes would be on Henry as the men waited to see if he would run again.

9

Wounded on the Field

Henry's indecision about what to do next isn't going to last long. If you look out to the woods, you'll see what I mean...

Henry stood in the road, still thinking about the men making fun of him. Suddenly, dark waves of Union soldiers swept out of the woods and down the fields. They charged past Henry like terrified buffaloes. Henry froze in horror, watching the men stampede away from the battlefield.

Henry tried to cry out. He wanted to give a speech, challenging the men to fight on, but all he could utter was, "Why...why, what's the matter?"

No one replied. The soldiers kept coming, and soon Henry was in the middle of a leaping, running mob. He kept repeating his question, but the burly men around him galloped along, as if he were invisible to them.

Cannons boomed in all directions as men kept darting across the field. The soldiers jabbered to themselves and each other. They were just spouting words that filled the air and mixed with the sound of trampling feet.

Henry continued to turn from one soldier to another, trying to find out what was happening. He reached out and grabbed one man by the arm.

"What happened? What's going—?" Henry tried to speak.

"Let me go!" the man screamed. "Let me go!"

The soldier's frenzy startled Henry. The man's eyes rolled as if out of control. He panted as he ran and tried to pull away from Henry, but Henry held onto him. The soldier dragged Henry along.

"Let me go!" the soldier repeated. "You hear me? Let me go!"

"Why...why—?" was all Henry could respond.

"All right, then!" the man shouted. He swung his rifle. It smashed into Henry's head. Henry's fingers fell weakly from the man's arm. His legs began to wobble, and tiny lightning bolts seemed to dance inside his eyes. His head filled with the deafening roar of thunder. The soldier bolted away, never looking back.

Henry staggered, his legs gave out, and he fell to the ground. Dazed, he lay there for a moment. He tried to stand. Pain, a crushing weight inside his skull, pinned him to the ground. He wrestled with the pain and kept trying to rise. Each time, the pain slammed him back down.

Finally, Henry slowly managed to get up on one

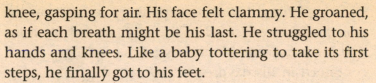

knee, gasping for air. His face felt clammy. He groaned, as if each breath might be his last. He struggled to his hands and knees. Like a baby tottering to take its first steps, he finally got to his feet.

He reached up and carefully touched his wound with his hand.

"Oww!" Henry howled, then hissed out a deep breath through clenched teeth. His fingers were stained blood-red. He stared at them.

The noises and actions of battle continued to swirl around him. A young officer on a white horse nearly ran over him. Guns, men, and horses all headed toward a gap in a nearby fence. Officers shouted orders, and the soldiers cursed and wailed. Henry, his head still spinning, saw the first hints of darkness in the sky.

As Henry stumbled away from the activity around him, the guns roared in the distance. They belched smoke and howled angrily, like demons guarding a gate. On the road, Henry saw overturned wagons. Dead horses and broken equipment littered both sides of the dirt path.

Henry's head slowly began to clear, and the pain gradually faded. He walked slowly, afraid to jerk about and stir up the agony all over again. His head felt swollen, almost too big for his neck to support. Blood trickled through his hair. As he walked he imagined himself back at the farm with his mother.

Oh, Mama's roast pork, Henry said to himself. *I can almost taste it.* **Oh! Me too!**

He pictured his mother putting the roast on the table as the sweet smell of the meat tickled his nose. *And her bread, and pie for dessert*, he continued in his daydream. Then he saw himself with his friends, swimming at the pond nearby. He felt the cool water all over his skin and could almost hear the maple leaves rustling in a summer breeze. Home seemed so far away. It was another world, so different from the sights and sounds of the battlefield.

The memories of home disappeared, and Henry felt his hazy head again. He shuffled along, barely able to pick up his feet.

"What should I do?" he mumbled to himself. "Just lie down here and sleep, or keep walking? Don't know what I should do."

His body ached all over, and the darkness clouded his vision. Suddenly, a cheery voice interrupted his thoughts.

"You seem to be in a pretty bad way, boy."

Henry didn't turn to speak to the man.

"Uh," was all he could say.

"Well," the cheery soldier said, "I'm going your way. Let me give you a hand." The soldier put his arm around Henry and held him steady. He asked Henry questions as they walked, and Henry mumbled a few words in reply.

"You say you're from the 304th Regiment?" the soldier asked. Henry nodded weakly.

"I didn't know they were fighting yet," the soldier said. "But I guess everyone got a taste of it today. It got pretty crazy out there. I could hardly tell which side I was fighting for. Thought for sure I was a dead man a few times, let me tell you. It'll be a miracle if we ever find our regiments tonight, eh?"

Henry listened closely to the man's bright voice. It was like a light of hope.

"I saw a good friend killed today," the soldier continued, his voice falling. "Jack was a nice fella. It really hurt to see him take a bullet. One minute he's standing there talking, the next he's hit—bang!—right in the side of the head. Tough thing to see."

Henry kept leaning on the man, trusting him to guide them through the woods. The man was like a hound following a scent, expertly moving around the trees and questioning the guards they met along the way. Finally, Henry saw an orange glow up ahead.

"See that fire?" the man asked. "That's your regiment."

Henry nodded.

"You'll be okay now. Good luck to you."

The soldier gave Henry a warm, strong handshake. Then he turned, whistling as he walked away. Henry realized, as the man melted into the darkness, that he had never seen the soldier's face.

There are all kinds of friendship. You have "close" friends, "best" friends, "canine" friends. There's also something called "the kindness of strangers." Even in the middle of that terrible war, a nameless soldier was willing to treat Henry kindly and help him to get to his regiment.

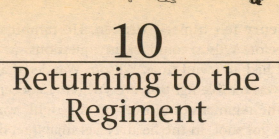

10
Returning to the Regiment

This is it—Henry finally has to face the men in his regiment. What will he tell them about where he's been and about his "red badge"?

Henry headed slowly toward the fire. How would he explain his wound? He didn't feel strong enough to make up a fancy tale. He could already hear the soldiers' taunts and insults if he told the truth. He thought about hiding in the woods, but he was too weak, too hungry, to go off by himself. He kept heading for the fire.

"Halt!" a soldier shouted in the darkness. Henry saw a rifle barrel gleam in the firelight. He paused, thinking he recognized the voice.

"Wilson?" Henry croaked weakly. "Hello, Wilson."

Wilson stepped forward and stared at Henry.

"Is that you, Henry?" Wilson asked.

"It's me."

"Well, what do you know." Wilson's voice softened and he chuckled a little. "It's good to see you, boy. I gave you up as a goner."

Henry felt himself weaken. He rambled out a story before Wilson could ask any questions.

"I had an awful time, Wilson. Wandered all over. There was terrible fighting everywhere. I got separated from the regiment, and over on the right, way over there, I got shot. In the head. Never imagined fighting so bad. Awful bad."

Wilson came closer. "What? Shot? Why didn't you say so right away? C'mon, I gotta get you some help."

A corporal named Simpson came over. "Another man come crawling back?" he asked Wilson. "That's forty-two of them so far. Is that Henry?"

"Yeah, it's Henry, and he's been shot," Wilson said. "We gotta take care of him." Wilson put his arm around Henry. "Must hurt like heck."

"Yeah, it does," Henry agreed. "It really does."

"Here, Henry, grab hold." The corporal offered his arm. "I'll help you."

Wilson stayed at his post. "Here, take my canteen. It's got some coffee. And put him in my blanket, Simpson," he called out as the two entered the camp. "When I get off guard duty, I'll come have a look at him."

Henry's injury deadened his senses. Wilson's voice sounded miles away, and he could barely feel Simpson's arm. He let the corporal steer him toward the fire.

"Now, let's take a look at that head," Simpson

said. He pushed Henry's hair out of the way and whistled when he saw the wound.

"Good Lord, what a strange-looking thing that is," Simpson said, shaking his head. "I bet you were just grazed by a bullet. Boy, you got some lump there. It's like someone took a big rock or something and smashed it against your skull."

Even as the pain made his head throb, Henry blushed as he remembered how he really got the wound. He stayed silent.

"It'll hurt even worse tomorrow, I bet you," Simpson went on. "But you'll be all right. You sit here and wait for Wilson. I gotta go check on the new guards coming on duty."

Henry nodded as Simpson went off into the darkness. He looked around and saw men lying on the ground or leaning against trees, sleeping. He heard the crackle of the fire and watched thin ribbons of smoke drift upward. Off to the right, Henry saw a handful of stars, tiny pebbles glowing against the black sky. He sat, not moving, until Wilson approached the fire.

"Okay, Henry, we're gonna fix you up now." Wilson handed Henry the canteen with coffee. Henry drank it greedily. The coffee was cool, and it slid easily down his dusty throat. Wilson took a handkerchief, soaked it in water, and put it on Henry's wound.

"There," Wilson said, tying a knot to keep the bandage in place. "You look awful, but I bet you feel better."

The cool cloth felt like his mother's tender hand on Henry's head. He smiled, grateful for Wilson's help.

"You're a tough one, Henry. Most men take a shot like that, they'd screech and squawk and rush right to the field hospital. A shot in the head's nothing to sneeze at."

Henry didn't say a word. Wilson was trying to make Henry sound brave. Henry didn't feel brave, and he didn't want to talk about the wound.

"C'mon, now," Wilson said, "get to bed. You need your rest."

Henry lay down under Wilson's blanket. The earth felt cool and soft. A deep sleep rushed over him.

Henry awoke feeling as if he had slept for a thousand years. A cold morning dew clung to his face, and he slid farther under his blanket. Already, gunfire was blasting in the distance. In the dim light, Henry saw the soldiers sleeping around him. Still foggy with sleep, he imagined for a moment that the men were dead bodies. But his mind cleared, he remembered where he was, and the horrible thought passed. These men weren't dead—not yet, anyway. But who knew what today's fighting would bring?

Hearing the fire snap and pop, Henry turned and saw Wilson throwing sticks into the red mouth of the flames. Henry stretched and yawned.

"So, Henry, how you feel?" Wilson asked with a smile.

Henry thought for a second, trying to measure his pain. "My head feels like a big, ripe melon," he said slowly. "And my stomach's churning something fierce. I guess I feel real bad."

"Looks like your bandage slipped," Wilson said. "Let me fix it for you."

Wilson pulled at the handkerchief and Henry gasped in pain.

"Gosh darn it!" Henry shouted. "Be careful! You act like you're nailing down a carpet with a ten-pound hammer!"

Wilson ignored Henry's anger. "Well, then, let's just leave it be for now and you can come over and get some grub." **Soldiers have a lot of slang names for food.**

Let's see...there's grub, chow, vittles...Say, is anyone else hungry?

Wilson got Henry some food and coffee. He watched with approval as Henry wolfed down the meal. As Henry ate he realized that Wilson had changed since they first met at training camp—even since just before the battle. The old Wilson was loud and always quick to argue. The soldier next to him now was thoughtful and generous. Wilson seemed more sure of himself, and he ignored the insults and jokes of the men around him. Had just one day's battle changed him so? Now, Henry thought, Wilson was really a man.

"Well, Henry," Wilson said, sipping from his coffee mug, "what do you think? Will we wallop them today?"

Henry smiled. "Two days ago, Wilson, you'd have said you could lick the whole Rebel army by yourself."

Wilson seemed surprised. "You think so? Well, maybe you're right." He fell silent. Henry felt bad. He had been teasing, but Wilson seemed bothered by the comment.

"Oh, no, you wouldn't have," Henry said.

"No, no, Henry, you're probably right. I was a pretty big fool sometimes."

They sat silently for a minute. Henry finally spoke up.

"Jim's dead," he said calmly. Death was just part of their life now.

"Jim Conklin?"

"I saw him, all tore up in the side."

"You don't say," Wilson said. "Poor Jim."

From a nearby campfire, angry voices suddenly rose. Two men were cursing each other, threatening to knock each other silly. Wilson stood up and went over to them.

"Hey, now, fellas, what's the use?" Wilson said pleasantly. "Save it for the Rebs. No need to fight with each other."

"Mind your own business," one of the men said coldly.

Wilson continued talking to them, trying to calm them down. After a minute, he returned to Henry.

"I hate to see the boys fighting like that."

"You have changed a good bit," Henry said with a laugh. "Before, you woulda been more than likely to jump into the fight yourself."

"I guess that's true," Wilson said thoughtfully. "I guess I really have changed."

There was another pause.

"The regiment lost over half the men yesterday," Wilson finally said. "I thought they was all dead. But just like you, they kept straggling back during the night. They'd been scattered all over, wandering through the woods, fighting with other regiments, and who knows what. Just like you."

Henry squirmed. "So?"

"Just saying, that's all."

Henry searched for something else to talk about—anything but yesterday and what he had done. He brushed his hand by his pocket and felt a bulge. It was the envelope Wilson had given him the day before. Henry had forgotten all about it.

Wilson had been so scared yesterday, he had thought about dying and wrapped up all his important things in that envelope. Only Henry knew how afraid Wilson had been. For a moment Henry felt he had a power over him. If Wilson started asking questions about the wound or about where Henry had gone, he could mention the envelope and Wilson's fears. Maybe Wilson would be so embarrassed he would stop being so nosy.

"Hey!"

Wilson's voice snapped Henry from his thoughts.

"Yeah?" Henry replied.

Wilson coughed and fidgeted.

"Well . . . ah . . . remember that envelope I gave you yesterday?"

"Yeah." Henry smiled to himself.

"Well, I guess you can give it back now."

"Oh, sure." Henry reached inside his coat and pulled out the packet. He handed it to Wilson, then looked away as he took it. Henry could feel his friend's embarrassment. Henry thought about making a joke or a comment, reminding Wilson of how afraid he had been, almost teary-eyed. But Henry remained quiet. It was the noble thing to do.

Wilson's face flushed as he stuffed the envelope into his pack.

You know, a little while ago, Henry might have poked fun at Wilson's embarrassment. But maybe the reality of war has changed his attitude a little. I wonder how else our young soldier is changing?

11
Henry the "Wildcat"

Henry seems very satisfied with himself. But he had visions of doing great things in battle once before, and the reality turned out differently. What will he really do the next time the fighting begins?

H enry never mentioned the envelope to Wilson again. He felt much better now. His pride was back. He stood with his legs spread wide, his arms folded across his chest, loaded with self-confidence. If he had made any mistakes, no one knew about them—or would ever know. As Henry thought about it he felt he'd done all right yesterday. He was a veteran now, a real soldier. He forgot all about the doubts and fears that had bothered him before.

Henry didn't worry about the next battle to come. He felt as if he could survive anything now. A little seed of self-confidence blossomed and grew within him. He had experienced more than most young men his age. He had faced the enemy dragons he had imagined. They weren't so deadly and fierce, after all. The dragon could not kill him. He, Henry Fleming, was chosen to do great things. He could still make his dreams of glory come true.

In his mind, Henry saw how the other men had run yesterday, throwing down their guns in fright. They had bolted off like crazed animals. He was sure he hadn't looked so foolish. He had run with dignity.

Henry forgot about yesterday for a moment and thought about the future. He imagined himself back home in New York, sitting in the living room in front of a huge fire. Friends and relatives were gathered around him as he talked about his days in the Union army.

The listeners sat with their mouths open, their eyes staring deeply into Henry's. They followed every tiny gesture he made. Each word he spoke made them hear the rumble of the cannons and see the blue and gray lines clashing in the field. They could feel Henry's heartbeat during the excitement of battle, and they cheered his bravery. He imagined his mother's shocked face as she heard about the dangers he had faced and the risks he had taken. Henry, the veteran soldier in this fantasy, glowed with satisfaction as he told his tales.

Gunfire shook Henry from his daydream. He smiled to himself, thinking about the scene he had pictured in his mind. Yesterday was just a fading memory.

The regiment began to move and then took positions behind a small hill. They waited again for the command to march forward. Some soldiers lay down with their backs to the fighting. Wilson, putting his head on his folded arms, quickly fell asleep.

Henry crouched behind the dirt pile and looked out. He saw trenches cut into the earth and the heads of soldiers bobbing above the ground. He heard many skirmishes all around, and off to the right, cannons roared. Talking was impossible.

At last, the guns fell silent. The men began to speak again, spreading rumors about the battles already fought and the action to come. Nothing anyone said cheered the troops. Everyone feared the worst. The men once again cursed the officers in charge. They had heard about too many captains and colonels who led their men to needless, crushing deaths.

"I swear," Henry joined in, "we've got a bunch of lunkheads for generals."

"You can say that again," a soldier nearby said with a nod.

Before long, the men started marching again. Wilson, still tired after his short nap, looked around. He yawned, then sighed.

"I suppose we'll get licked today," he said sadly.

Henry ignored him. He continued to attack the generals and their decisions. Wilson did not join in.

"You know, Henry, maybe they're doing the best they know how. Maybe it's just our luck to get beat." Wilson sagged. He looked as if someone had beaten the strength out of his body.

"Well, don't we fight like the devil?" Henry demanded. "Don't we do all that men can do?"

Suddenly, he looked away. He felt guilty for saying that. Yesterday, he hadn't done all that he could. But no one else knew that. None of the soldiers

gave him dirty looks as he made his speech. Henry's courage returned.

"One officer said he never saw a new regiment fight like we did," Henry went on. "We fought as good as anyone, don't you think?"

"Sure, sure we did," Wilson replied. "Nobody can call us quitters or cowards. But still . . . we just don't get any luck."

"Well, if we're fighting well, and we keep losing, it's got to be the generals' fault," Henry said, sure of himself.

A soldier behind him heard these comments. "I guess," he said slowly, "you think you fought the whole battle by yourself yesterday, eh, Fleming?"

The words cut into Henry. He felt like a child caught telling a lie.

"Well, no," Henry mumbled. "'Course I don't think I fought the whole battle yesterday." Could the man know? Had he seen Henry run off yesterday? No—he accepted Henry's humble response.

"Oh," the man replied, still teasing Henry with the tone of his voice. "I see."

Henry was relieved the conversation was over. But his fear remained, fear that somehow the men would learn what he had done. Henry decided to keep quiet.

The men continued to gossip as they marched along. Gunfire rang out around them. The men cursed every time the shots grew louder. The regiment stopped when it reached a field. Henry heard the men grumbling and swearing, and their anger fueled his own.

"I tell you, Wilson," he growled. "It don't make sense the way they march us about. We're like squirrels being hounded by a dog, running this way and that. Nobody knows where we're going or why we're going there."

"Squirrels? I love chasing squirrels."

"Easy, Henry," Wilson said.

But Henry kept going. "We marched into those woods and didn't do a darn thing except make ourselves a target for those guns. It makes me sick. We got tangled up in the prickers and branches and then the Rebs had an easy time of it. You talk about luck, but it's not bad luck that's our problem, it's these—"

"Everything will be fine, Henry," Wilson interrupted, speaking calmly. "You'll see."

"How can you talk like that?" Henry exploded. "Don't tell me. I know—"

The lieutenant stiffly walked down the line of soldiers.

"You boys just shut up!" he barked. "I'm sick of all this jabbering and complaining. You're here to fight, not talk, and you'll see plenty of fighting any minute. So, just keep your mouths shut."

He stopped, waiting for anyone to dare to speak. Henry and the others were silent. The lieutenant

stormed off. In a minute, his words proved true. Sounds of battle grew louder, drew closer. The men got ready for a Rebel charge. The Union cannons began to fire, responding to the Southern guns. The men, exhausted from marching, worn down from war, slowly took their positions.

Henry felt a burning hate for the Rebs pulsing through his body. The Rebs never seemed to slow; they just fought on. He hated the Rebs today the way he had hated the whole world yesterday. The hatred burned hotter than a thousand campfires. Henry felt like a wild animal backed into a corner. Once trapped, the beast shows its true strength, sprouting fangs and claws.

Like that trapped animal, Henry snarled. He swallowed, trying to control the rage squeezing his stomach. He fingered his rifle nervously. In his anger, he thought of the vicious, terrible things he would do if he ever got his hands on a Reb.

One rifle in the regiment fired, then another. In an instant, the whole regiment was firing. Gunshots slashed through the smoke hanging above the field. But the Rebs kept coming. Henry imagined they sensed victory. He hated them even more now and wanted to take his fists and smash the smiles off their grinning faces.

Henry lost all sense of where he was and what he was doing. He lost his balance and fell. *Have I been hit?* he asked himself. But then he realized that he was all right, and he jumped up.

He stood behind a tree and fired his rifle again
and again. The barrel grew hot; it seemed almost to
glow like the wooden coals in a campfire. Henry barely
noticed. He reloaded and fired without thinking, his
anger shooting out with each shot. He grunted as he
pulled the trigger, as if he were punching someone
with all his might.

When the Union troops moved forward, Henry
was in the front. When they were forced back, Henry
did it slowly, not wanting to give ground. He kept
firing, and when all the other soldiers around him
stopped, Henry kept firing.

"Fleming, that's enough," a voice cried with
amazement. "Can't you see there's nothing to shoot at?"

Henry lowered his rifle and looked around him, as if in a dream. The other soldiers stared at him, awed by how he had fought. Finally, he seemed to wake up and saw that the Rebs had retreated through the smoke.

"Oh," he said meekly. His throat burned. His whole body seemed strangely on fire; he threw himself on the ground, as if to put out a blaze.

Above Henry, the lieutenant passed by. He seemed elated with the success of the battle.

"Fleming, that was some good fighting! If I had ten thousand wildcats like you, I could crush those Rebels in a week."

The other soldiers pointed at Henry and whispered about his wild, unstoppable fighting. They had never seen a soldier so filled with rage.

Wilson staggered over.

"Are you all right, Henry? Do you feel okay? I never seen you like that before."

"I'm fine," Henry gasped. His throat was still too hot to let him speak. Henry finally realized what he had done. He was now a hero.

"Good work, good work," the lieutenant praised him again. The other men joined in and congratulated themselves on their performance too.

But the sound of guns still clattered. There was more to come.

What a difference from yesterday's battle! Henry was swept away by the excitement of battle. But what will happen as the fighting continues?

12
The Insult

THE RED BADGE OF COURAGE may have been based on a real battle—the Battle of Chancellorsville. In just that one battle, about thirty thousand men were killed, wounded, or missing. That number is almost too big to comprehend, but each of those soldiers had his own story. Henry has already heard some of those stories from the soldiers he has encountered. But what about the officers who run the war? What do they think of the men they command?

The soldiers rested for a moment, glad for the break in the fighting. As the gunfire died down Henry heard one of his comrades crying in pain. The wounded man may have been injured for quite a while; Henry couldn't tell. The roar of the cannons would have drowned out his shouts. Now, though, everyone could hear his cries.

"Who is it?" Wilson asked.

"Could be Jimmie Rogers," Henry said. "Sounds like Jimmie."

The two friends went over to the wounded man. They pulled back when they saw him. Rogers was rolling on the ground, his arms and legs thrashing wildly.

"Help me! Help me! It hurts, hurts so bad!" Rogers's words cut through Henry like a sword. The pain made his voice rough and raw. "Don't just stand there! I'm shot, can't you see it? It *hurts*!"

"I, I'll get you some water to wash out the wound," Wilson finally said. "There's a stream over to the left just a little ways."

Wilson grabbed his canteen. Other soldiers threw their empty canteens to him, asking him to refill them with water. With canteens dangling all over his body, Wilson set off. Henry followed him.

"I'm sure it's over this way," Wilson said, hunting for the stream. But after a few minutes, with no luck finding it, they gave up.

Here, a little way from the battle, Henry got a better look at what was happening. Soldiers moved along the roads, and in the fields cannons flared, making gray clouds. Great flashes of orange flames blasted through the smoke. Henry saw that the roof of a lone house not too far away had been hit, and a tower of smoke rose from it into the sky.

Henry noticed groups of Union soldiers forming into regiments and brigades. Behind them, a line of soldiers retreated down a dusty lane like so many ants heading back to their hill. Smoke rose above all this action, and guns fired constantly.

Bullets screeched by Henry and Wilson as they made their way through the woods. They passed wounded men and other soldiers picking their way

through the trees and brush. Looking down a row of trees, Henry saw an injured man crawling on his hands and knees. A general and his assistant, a brigadier general, rode toward the man. They ignored the soldier. The general moved his horse carefully around him, as if he were a dead animal in the road. One of the injured man's arms gave out, and he collapsed on the forest floor. He rolled over on his back and lay there, not moving.

Henry and Wilson crouched behind a tree, waiting to see what would happen next. The general rode on. He stopped just a few feet in front of Henry and Wilson, who were hidden from his view by the

brush. The general's assistant halted beside his commander.

"We should go back," Wilson whispered to Henry.

"Yeah," Henry said. "But first let's try to hear what they say." He pointed toward the two officers. "Could be real important. Don't let 'em see you."

Henry knew who this general was. He commanded many regiments, including Henry's. Henry listened closely to the officers' words.

"The enemy's forming for another charge." The general spoke coolly, as if he were talking about tomorrow's weather. "They might break through this time if we don't stop them."

The assistant paused before answering.

"I don't know, sir. It'll be tough to beat them here."

"I know."

The two officers lowered their voices. Henry saw them gesture, pointing one way, then another, but he couldn't hear their words. Finally, the general raised his voice again.

"What troops can you spare?" he asked.

"Well, sir, the 12th Regiment is over helping the 76th. We're pretty tight right now." The officer paused. "There is the 304th—"

"The 304th!" Henry whispered to Wilson. "That's us!"

"—but you know, sir, they fight like a bunch of mule drivers. Still, they're all we have free right now."

Henry and Wilson stared at each other, their mouths open in astonishment.

"Well, get them ready," the general said. "I'll send a message when it's time to start them. Probably in a few minutes."

The brigadier general saluted and started to turn his horse. The commanding general spoke again.

"Don't expect too many of your 'mule drivers' to make it back."

Wilson and Henry looked at each other again. They both had the same frightened expression. As the officer rode off, the two soldiers hurried back to their regiment. Henry knew they had been gone only a few minutes, but it felt like days, even months. He felt that he had suddenly grown old. He saw the war with new eyes. He knew something he had never truly realized before: He was very insignificant.

The officers talked about the regiment as if it were a wooden broom, not a group of living men. That's it, Henry realized, they were just a broom, and the general wanted to sweep something away. If the broom broke, he would just send for another one. Were all leaders like this? Henry wondered. Was all war like this?

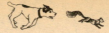

Henry and Wilson stumbled back to camp, eager to share their news. The lieutenant greeted them angrily.

"Fleming! Wilson! How long does it take to get water?"

"We're gonna charge!" Wilson blurted. "We're gonna charge!"

"Charge," the lieutenant said, pleased. "Well, what do you know. This will be some real fighting!" He smiled. "Charge. Well, that's more like it!"

The word spread up and down the ranks.

"Charge?"

"Wilson and Fleming say we're gonna charge."

"Charge? What for?"

"Wilson, you're lying," one soldier challenged.

Henry stepped up. "He ain't lying. We both heard the general give the order."

"That's right," Wilson said. "The general and another officer were talking. We're gonna charge."

The men saw an officer ride over to their colonel. It was the brigadier general. Henry pointed at him.

"That's it," Wilson said. "That's the order coming now."

The men nodded. It was true—the regiment was going to charge. As the idea sank in, the men hitched up their pants and straightened their caps, thinking about what it meant.

The regiment's officers quickly began herding the men into a tight formation. They acted like shepherds tending their sheep. The soldiers peered ahead at the field they were about to cross. The rumble of cannon fire filled their ears. Henry looked over at his friend.

"Mule drivers," Henry whispered.

"'Not many will make it back," Wilson said.

Only they knew how the officers really felt about their regiment. Only they knew the dangers ahead. And yet they saw no hesitation in each other's face. Wilson looked at Henry and said, "We're gonna get swallowed."

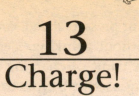

13
Charge!

Henry now understands what the generals think of men like him. Maybe the insult has made Henry less likely to fight bravely. Or maybe the words have stirred Henry to prove he's not a "mule driver" after all.

Henry stared ahead and wondered what waited for them in the woods across the field. Out of the corner of his eye, he saw an officer waving his hat.

"That's it," Wilson said. "That's the signal."

The men began to move. Henry felt soldiers behind him push and jostle as he tried to get up to speed. Finally, his legs began to pump, and he was running.

Henry headed for a clump of trees ahead. He imagined the Rebs hiding there. He ran as if he were being chased by a raging bear. The skin on his face felt tight, and his eyes burned with a devilish glare. With his dirty face and clothes, his bloodstained bandage, and his gear swinging wildly on his body, Henry looked like a madman.

The regiment pressed ahead, cutting through trees and bushes. Without thinking, Henry had taken the lead in his little band of charging soldiers. He heard the Rebs yelling as the Union troops approached. Bullets flew, and a shell exploded in the middle of a group of soldiers nearby. The blast threw one man skyward, his arms covering his bloody red face. The Confederate bullets began hitting their targets, and blue-coated bodies fell all around.

It seemed to Henry that he saw every single detail. Each blade of the green grass was bold and clear. He saw each swirl and bump in the brown bark of the trees he passed. He saw and understood everything that was happening.

Men on both sides shouted in anger and confusion. They were like a wild mob with an unstoppable will to fight, no matter how close to death they might be. But after a while, the Union troops began to slow. The superhuman strength and energy the soldiers had at the beginning of their charge now drained from them. They were just regular men, after all.

As soon as the regiment slowed, the enemy fire became a steady roar. The men could see the work of the Rebel bullets and shells: Dead Union soldiers were scattered all over the battleground. More men fell, dying with screams of pain. The remaining troops stared blankly at the destruction all around them. Henry saw fear in the faces of his fellow soldiers. For a

moment, the men seemed paralyzed, even as the war raged around them.

"What are you doing, you fools!" the lieutenant finally bellowed. "You'll be killed for sure if you just stand there!" The lieutenant kept shouting, but another round of cannon fire muffled his words.

"Come on!" he shouted again.

The men didn't move. The lieutenant began to curse. Henry had never heard a man swear like that before. The words seemed to stir Wilson. He dropped to one knee and fired his rifle. The sound shook the other men to life. They no longer huddled like aimless sheep. The troops remembered their purpose, and they shouldered their guns and began to move forward again. They stopped every few feet, fired, reloaded, then inched forward again.

The enemy fire was like a wall now. Smoke blocked Henry's vision. He tried to see through it, to see what was waiting on the other side. An open space stood between his regiment and the Rebel troops. They stopped again, taking cover behind some trees. Some of the men were wide-eyed, amazed by the terrible battle all around them. They no longer seemed to understand where they were or what they should do next.

The lieutenant began to yell and swear again. He ignored the bullet that sailed by his head as he moved among the men, trying to get them to advance.

"Come on, you lunkheads!" the lieutenant

roared. "Come on! We'll get killed if we stay here. We've got to get across that field!"

"Cross here?" Henry asked him in disbelief.

"Of course! Come on! We can't stay here."

"Come on yourself," Henry snapped. His tone surprised them both. "You go too," he challenged the officer.

Without saying a word, the lieutenant accepted Henry's dare. He set off down the line with Henry by his side, calling to the other men. Wilson quickly joined them.

"Come on!" they yelled, waving their arms. "Come on!"

The flag seemed to follow the men's order. It began to blow straight ahead. Slowly, the men responded to the cry. The regiment began to surge forward.

Yellow tongues of fire shot out of the Rebel cannons. Thick blue smoke hung above the Union men. Sounds were lost in the mighty roar of gunfire.

Henry raced across the field to the nearby woods. He tucked his head low and pumped his legs fiercely. His eyes were partly closed, and everything around him was a fuzzy blur.

Henry looked up briefly and saw the Union flag. The flag bearer was charging across the field, too,

The flag-bearer is the soldier who carries the flag in battle.

crouching low and zigzagging to avoid Rebel bullets. Henry felt something stir inside, a new love for the familiar red, white, and blue. The flag seemed to have a deep power, the power to protect all living things around it. Henry stayed close to it.

Suddenly, the flag dipped. The flag bearer had been hit. He trembled, then fell. Henry grabbed the flagpole. At almost the same instant, Wilson reached for it from the other side. They pulled at it, but the dead flag bearer's hands still held it tightly. It was as if even in death he still knew how special the flag was. Finally, the two friends wrestled the pole from the dead man's hands. Wilson and Henry held the banner high.

"Give it to me!" Henry said.

"No, I've got it," Wilson said.

They knew that whoever carried the flag would risk being an obvious target for the enemy. Henry pushed Wilson away and grabbed the flag.

14
Henry Leads the Way

Henry now has the flag, and he holds it proudly. But around him, the battle is not going so well. . . .

The regiment fell back to a line of trees. The soldiers fired at the Rebs, who came rushing forward. The Union troops slowly snaked through the trees. The regiment had been hit hard; dead and wounded littered the battlefield. When the men reached the open field again, countless rounds of enemy gunfire met them.

Henry could see that the men were exhausted, weary from the battle and their heavy casualties. His comrades marched with bowed heads, meekly accepting the rain of bullets. The men, Henry sensed, felt they were fighting an unbeatable foe. Their hatred for the officers who led them boiled up again, staining their faces a flushed red.

But at the rear of the Union line, a few men still loaded their rifles and fired at the Rebs. They had not given up. Leading these men was the young lieutenant. He still swore and screamed and begged the men to fight on. His right arm, clipped by a Rebel bullet, hung straight at his side.

Henry couldn't bear to see the regiment falling apart. He wanted to show the general and the brigadier general that he and his comrades weren't "mule drivers." He hoped that the men would fight bravely and well and that the officers would be embarrassed by their insult. But that dream, like so many others, had been destroyed, crushed by the Rebel guns. Henry felt shame rush through him as he watched his fellow mule drivers retreat.

Henry tried to get back his pride. He held the flag straight and high. He yelled at his comrades, pleading with them to fight on.

"Jones, Barton," he called, saying the name of every man he knew. "C'mon, we can still lick 'em!"

Henry pushed on their chests with his free hand, as if he could shove them into action. He and the lieutenant kept up their cries, stirring the men to fight. Henry felt that he and the lieutenant shared a special relationship now. They encouraged each other with their shouts.

But the regiment was like a run-down machine. Henry and the lieutenant couldn't get the men going again. A few soldiers moved forward, but stopped as they saw others around them slipping back away from the fighting. The wounded lay where they had fallen, crying for help.

Smoke and flames surrounded them. Looking through a gap in the haze, Henry saw the Rebs ahead.

With wild yells, they fired their guns at the retreating Union soldiers. Some of Henry's comrades returned the gunfire. Henry's ears buzzed with shots and screams.

The Union troops seemed confused, not knowing which way they should go.

"That's our line over there," one soldier said. "Why are we getting shot at by our own men?"

"Can't be," another said. "It must be the Rebs."

Men ran in all directions, filled with panic. They tried to find safe places to hide. All the while, the Confederate bullets kept coming.

Henry stood there holding the flag. He breathed in huge amounts of smoky air, almost choking on it. Wilson came over to him.

"W-well, Henry," he stuttered, "I-I guess this is it."

"Oh, shut up, you fool!" Henry refused to admit defeat. He looked away from his friend.

The officers tried to regroup the men so they could defend themselves against this latest Rebel attack. Soldiers fell to their stomachs, nestling into craters in the ground. Others ducked for cover behind trees. Everyone sought safety from the whistling bullets.

"Here they come!" the lieutenant cried. "Right at us!"

The rest of his bold speech was drowned out by the thunder of guns.

Through the smoke, Henry saw how close the

advancing Rebs were. He could pick out features on their faces—a flat nose, an open mouth. Their gray uniforms, trimmed with bright red cloth, seemed new. They moved cautiously, not exactly sure how close they were to the Union troops.

The lieutenant's cry roused the men to action. Now the Union soldiers fired into the Rebs. The smoke from the guns hid the Rebs from Henry's view. He sensed that each side was firing, like two boxers standing toe-to-toe, trading heavy blows.

Henry sat down gloomily with the flag between his legs.

"Well," he muttered to himself, "if we gotta go down, at least we're going down fighting."

But his comrades were doing better than Henry realized. Fewer Reb bullets came blasting at them. The smoke began to clear, and the regiment looked out in amazement. The Rebs were gone! All that remained in front of them were a few gray-coated corpses, twisted and mangled.

"Do you believe it?" one man said. "We drove 'em off."

"Yes sir," another soldier gushed, "we sure did."

The whole regiment began to whoop and cheer. A few even did little dances of victory.

So far, Henry thought, the regiment had fought a string of tiny battles. Most of them had seemed to end in failure. But this time the men had won. For the first time in a long while, Henry felt the troops glow with pride. They had redeemed themselves. With their guns in their hands, they could do anything. They were men.

Sometimes, you have to reach way down inside yourself to find the strength to keep going. It can happen in sports, or school, or work, or any really tough challenge. And when you can do it, when you can accomplish something that looked impossible—well, it's a great feeling.

And I imagine Henry and his fellow Union soldiers are feeling that way right now...

15
A Job Well Done

Sometimes it seems that Henry and the men have been fighting forever. But remember, this is just Henry's second day in battle. Now there's a break in the action, and the troops can rest for a moment.

Cannons still fired in the distance, but in front of Henry and his comrades everything was still. The men sighed with relief and huddled together as they marched away. Some looked back over their shoulders, as if they expected a sudden attack from the rear. *It would be ironic*, Henry thought, *to survive a battle, then die from a stray bullet while everything seemed so peaceful.*

The men headed past their own lines. A regiment resting under some trees began to tease the weary soldiers.

"What are you doing?" one of the resting soldiers called. "Think you're going home now?"

Another shouted, "Was it hot out there today, boys?"

"Oh, mama," teased a third soldier, "come out and see the pretty soldiers."

A red-bearded officer began to shout back at the taunting men, and a soldier near Henry challenged someone to a fight. The lieutenant, however, stepped in and calmed the rising tensions.

How could they talk like that? Henry questioned himself, his anger boiling. *Didn't we just hold off the Rebs?* His hatred for the mocking soldiers burned as if they were the enemy too. Henry looked around and saw many of the men in his regiment walking with heavy steps, as if they were ashamed.

They marched back to the position they had held before their charge. Henry now realized how little ground they had covered. And the fighting, which he thought had gone on for hours, actually had taken just a few minutes. Maybe the mocking soldiers were right after all. The regiment hadn't done anything special.

Henry watched his comrades guzzle water from their canteens. For the first time, he could sit back and think about what he had done. The memory made him feel light and happy. He had done well.

This pleasant thought disappeared as Henry saw an officer ride up. It was the brigadier general, the one who had first called them mule drivers. The officer's face was tight with anger. Even his movements, the way he jerked his horse to a stop, showed his rage. He halted by the regiment's colonel.

"What were you doing out there, MacChesnay?" the brigadier general roared. "You really made a mess of things. Good Lord, man, you stopped a hundred feet short of giving the Rebs a real kick in the pants! A hundred feet more and it would have been a great charge. Instead . . ." The brigadier general took a deep breath, then began again. "I tell you, you've got a bunch of mule drivers out there, and sorry, good-for-nothing mud diggers, not soldiers!"

The men looked at MacChesnay, their colonel, waiting for him to respond. They hoped he'd blast right back at the other officer.

"Well, sir," the colonel said, "we went as far as we could."

"As far as you could? Well, by God, it wasn't far enough. You were supposed to draw the Rebs away from the fighting over there," the brigadier general said as he stabbed the air with his arm. "Can you hear the fighting going on there now? I'd say you did a pretty poor job of it, Colonel."

The brigadier general didn't wait for a reply. He turned sharply and rode away.

Standing next to the colonel, the lieutenant steamed.

"I don't care who he is," the lieutenant said. "He's a fool if he thinks our boys didn't fight well."

"Lieutenant," the colonel said slowly, "if you please. He is one of our commanders."

"All right, sir, all right." The lieutenant sat down. Slowly, the word spread through the ranks that the brigadier general had criticized their fighting. At first, the men grumbled angrily. But then they started to think that maybe the officer was right. Wilson, however, couldn't accept that.

"That man must be blind if he didn't see the way we fought," Wilson said. "What does he think, we were out there playing marbles?"

"Oh, he probably didn't see anything at all and thinks we're just a bunch of lost sheep," Henry said calmly. "He's just mad we didn't do what he wanted us to do. Just our bad luck."

"Bad luck is right," Wilson said. "What's the point in fighting for a bunch of officers who don't appreciate what you do for them? No matter what, we can't do anything to please 'em. Next time, let 'em make the charge themselves. I'll just sit and watch."

Henry tried to soothe Wilson. "Well, no matter what, we know we did good. Nobody can say anything against the two of us."

"No sir, they can't," Wilson quickly agreed. "I even heard one fella say that we two were the best in the regiment. Another fella jumped up and said it was a lie, said he never seen us fight at all. But some other boys defended us, and pretty soon there was a big argument about how we fought. But to have to listen to the brigadier general, it just makes me crazy!"

"He's a lunkhead," Henry said suddenly. "I wish he'd be there next time. We'd show him who's a mule driver or a mud digger."

A small group of soldiers approached Henry and Wilson. The men bounced with excitement.

"Hey, Fleming," one said, " you gotta hear this."

"Hear what?" Henry asked.

"We were standing by the lieutenant, and the colonel came over," the soldier said. "'Lieutenant Hasbrouck,' the colonel says, 'who was that lad carrying our flag?' The lieutenant, he doesn't waste a second, he says, 'Fleming, sir. Good young man. Fights like the devil.' Then the colonel says, 'Well yes, he's a good fella. He kept the flag out front. He did a good job. He's a good soldier to have.'"

Wilson looked approvingly at Henry. Henry was silent with pleasant surprise.

"And Wilson," the soldier bubbled on, "the lieutenant mentioned you too. He says, 'Fleming and Wilson, the two of them, were at the head of the charge hollering like Indians.' And the colonel says, 'Wilson, eh? Well, Lieutenant, those two deserve to be major generals.' Yup, that's what he said, 'major generals.'"

Wilson and Henry shook their heads after hearing all this good news.

"Ah, you're lying," Wilson said.

"I don't believe it," Henry protested, though not strongly. He and Wilson both glowed with pride, knowing deep down that the soldier was telling the truth. Henry and his friend exchanged smiles of congratulations.

All the complaints Henry and Wilson had just voiced faded away. Their hearts danced with joy. Henry felt as if he could take on the whole Rebel army all by himself. But the two friends couldn't enjoy the praise for long. Henry looked up and saw, once again, Rebel troops pouring out of the woods like gray swirling waters flooding the landscape.

16
Victory!

Henry and Wilson have finally earned their much deserved praise from the commanding officers. They feel like big dogs now, but will that be enough to get them through their toughest battle yet? Charge!

As the enemy approached, Henry felt a serene self-confidence. He smiled briefly as he watched the Union troops dodge and duck the bullets and shells flying toward them. He stood straight and tall as he looked over the field, and a calmness washed over him. Other regiments ahead began to move, while Henry's remained farther back. All around him, Henry saw clashes between blue and gray soldiers. Two Rebel units fought two Northern units; the gunfire was rapid and strong.

Off to the left, a Union brigade dashed into the forest, going after the Rebels. The trees blocked Henry's view, but he could hear the sounds of battle rising above the trees. In a field farther away, waves of blue trampled over gray. The men screamed and yelled like maniacs as they charged.

The 304th Regiment had lost a lot of men. Still, Henry and his comrades were ready to fight when their time came. As the bullets zeroed in on them the soldiers shouted in rage and pain. They loaded their rifles, slamming the bullets in and ramming them down with their steel rods. The guns fired in puffs of gray that swirled around the soldiers' heads. Flashes of yellow and red cut through the heavy smoke.

Henry stood with the flag, soaking up every detail of the battle around him. The Rebs moved closer; Henry saw their faces straining as they ran. The Rebs took cover behind a fence and fired mercilessly at the regiment. Union troops dropped to the ground.

No matter what, Henry said to himself, *I ain't moving. I'll die here if I have to.*

That would be his revenge, Henry thought. He would show the officers that he wasn't a mule driver or a mud digger. The brigadier general's comments still fueled Henry's anger, like a huge log stoking a fire. Maybe the officer would feel sorry, Henry thought, if he saw Henry's lifeless body on the ground, with flagpole still clutched in his grimy hands.

Men fell all around Henry as bullets ripped into their bodies. Some collapsed with loud, painful screams. Others tumbled silently to the ground. A sergeant nearby took a shot in the jaw. His mouth fell open, and Henry saw a bloody mass of teeth and flesh. The sergeant fled to the rear. Other men took bullets in the arms and legs and tried to crawl to safety.

Henry searched for Wilson. He saw his friend covered with gunpowder. The lieutenant was still scrambling among the men, a bandage shielding his wounded arm. He cursed louder than ever. But even his pleas couldn't keep the troops going. Men continued to drop, and the regiment's firing weakened.

The colonel rode up to the back of the line.

"We must charge again!" he shouted. "We must charge!"

Other officers riding behind the colonel repeated his order. Henry studied how far away the Rebs were.

"We could do it," Henry whispered to himself. "Heck, if we don't try it, they'll slaughter us right here."

But could the weary men manage another assault? Henry was surprised to see the soldiers quickly preparing to charge. They placed their bayonets on their rifles, and in a few seconds, the regiment was ready.

"Charge!" the colonel yelled.

The men shouted and sprang forward in eager leaps. It was a surprising burst of energy, Henry thought, after all the fighting they had already done. The dusty swarm of tattered soldiers raced across a green field under a light blue sky. Soon, the red of blood would color this picture. The regiment raced for the fence, where the Rebs' guns were blazing smoke and hot lead.

Henry was in front again, holding the flag high. He waved his free arm and shouted encouragement, but the men didn't need it. They were racing forward with all their strength and speed, ignoring the gunfire around them. They were ready to give their lives. That same brave, unselfish spirit filled Henry. He would keep going no matter how many Confederate guns fired in his face.

Henry's body and mind were tight with tension. Smoke hid the fence that protected the gray men behind it. Henry imagined there would be a loud crash when the running Union troops hit the Rebs.

But the collision of bodies never came. The Rebs, seeing the wild charging mob of the regiment, feeling its hot anger, began to run. One or two Rebs turned to fire back at the Union troops, but most fled as fast as they could. A small group of Rebs, however, didn't run. They gathered around a tree near the fence and kept shooting. Their flag waved proudly above them.

The Union regiment focused all its hatred on these remaining Rebels. The men bared their teeth and lunged at their enemy. Henry looked at the Rebel flag.

"I've got to get it," he said.

The flag would be a great prize, Henry thought. The generals had their medals that they earned for bravery in battle. The Rebel flag would be his sign of honor. He had to have it. He ran like a wild horse, heading for the flag, holding his own banner high above him as he ran.

The rest of the regiment stopped its charge and fired. Rebel soldiers fell. The Union troops ran forward again to continue their attack. Henry saw four or five Rebels standing by the flag. One, the flag bearer, was clutching his chest. Blood poured from the deadly wound and ran between his fingers. The man struggled to stand, as if he were fighting invisible demons trying to drag him down. He held the flag tight to his body even as he stumbled and staggered about.

The regiment was at the fence, climbing over it,

cheering wildly. The wounded flag bearer continued his dance of death, his free arm flailing about. His eyes filled with despair as the Union troops came toward him.

Wilson climbed the fence and headed for the flag bearer, beating Henry to the man. Like a panther, Wilson leapt at the Confederate soldier and pulled the flag from the bearer's beefy hands. Once he had it, Wilson held the flag high over his head and shouted with joy. The red banner snapped in the wind. The flag bearer made one last grab at his prized possession. Then he stiffened and fell to the ground, his face

buried in the soft green grass that was now soaked with his blood.

All around, the Union troops wildly celebrated their victory. They laughed and shouted and gestured gleefully. They threw their caps into the air and stamped their feet.

Four Confederate prisoners stood glumly to the side. The Union men looked at them closely, as if they were strange birds from a faraway land. One prisoner was wounded in the foot. In terrible pain, the man held the foot while he loudly cursed his captors.

Another prisoner was just a boy, even younger than Henry. He didn't seem nervous. He spoke calmly with his enemy, talking about the battles they had fought against each other. A third prisoner stared coldly at the Union troops. Whenever a soldier approached, he snarled with rage. The fourth prisoner sat silently. Henry imagined the shame the man felt at failing in battle.

The victory celebration went on. Some men shot their guns off into the distance, aiming at imaginary targets. Wilson and Henry sat down next to each other. Henry propped his flag against the fence. Wilson did the same with the captured Rebel flag.

"We did it, Henry" Wilson said, a smile lighting up his face.

"Yup," Henry agreed, beaming at his friend. "We really did."

17
From Boy to Man

What a battle! With courage and a lot of determination, Henry Fleming has grown from a scared young boy running from a fight into a full-fledged, flag-bearing Union soldier. And in only two days! I wonder how Henry feels about everything that has happened?

The sound of guns slowly began to fade. Once in a while, the rumble of cannon fire broke the spreading quiet. Soldiers moved about, carrying equipment and pushing cannons.

"Well now, what do you think?" Henry asked Wilson.

"I bet we'll go back the way we came, over by the river," his friend replied.

They sat silently, waiting for an order. In a moment they learned that Wilson was right—the regiment was going to return the way it came. The men stood up slowly, stretching their weary arms and legs. They marched back over the field they had just run across so wildly as they shouted their cries of war. The regiment joined up with the rest of the brigade, and the long, thin blue line of dust-covered troops headed through the woods back to the road.

The men walked beside the winding river. Henry looked back at the battlefield one last time. He studied the trampled grass and the battered, useless equipment that dotted the field. He took a breath and nudged Wilson.

"Well, I guess it's over," Henry said.

Wilson turned back too. "Yup, it really is."

Henry thought about what the last two days had meant. He had been surrounded by gunfire and smoke and death—and he had survived. And not just survived. Henry remembered all the great things he had done. He had stepped up during the battle and fought wildly. He had bravely carried the flag in battle. Others had seen Henry's courage and praised him. He knew he should be proud of his deeds.

But then Henry remembered the other things he had done. He saw himself running from the first battle and hiding in the woods. And he remembered the tattered soldier. Even though the poor man had been dying, he had tried to help Jim Conklin and had worried about Henry's wound. And Henry had been too ashamed to admit he wasn't hurt at all. Then, Henry had left the wounded tattered man by himself in the field.

A cold sweat broke out on Henry's forehead. What if Wilson could read his thoughts? Would the other soldiers know what Henry had done? Would they ever find out that he had lied about being shot, that he had been afraid to explain how he got his red badge of courage?

Henry cried out faintly.

Wilson turned. "Is something wrong, Henry?"

Henry swore softly, not wanting to answer the question.

The men around him talked about the battle they had just fought and the battles to come. Henry kept quiet, remembering how he had fled. All he could see in his mind was the dying tattered soldier. He would carry that image forever.

Henry thought back to his earlier ideas about war. He despised them now, knowing how wrong they were. He knew the truth about war and about himself. Henry felt strong inside. He had confidence in who he was and what he could do. Henry had learned about death, and he had survived. He was a man.

Henry's dreams about war didn't come true. But he was able to make the best of it after he faced his own fears. It's like those golden rays of sunlight cutting through the clouds—Henry found darkness and light, good and bad, mixed together. And he learned that's what life is really like.

As for me, I've finally made it out of the woods. And the only thing left for this army dog to do is to get some grub. Dinnertime! Let's MOVE OUT!

A little dog with a big imagination!^{SM}

WISHBONE™

Let television's canine hero be your tour guide...

and don't miss any of the WISHBONE™ retellings of these classic adventures!

Each WISHBONE™ book only $3.99!

DON QUIXOTE • Miguel de Cervantes
THE ODYSSEY • Homer
ROMEO & JULIET • William Shakespeare
JOAN OF ARC • Mark Twain
OLIVER TWIST • Charles Dickens
THE ADVENTURES OF ROBIN HOOD
FRANKENSTEIN • Mary Shelley
THE STRANGE CASE OF DR. JEKYLL AND MR. HYDE
• Robert Louis Stevenson
A JOURNEY TO THE CENTER OF THE EARTH • Jules Verne
THE RED BADGE OF COURAGE • Stephen Crane
THE ADVENTURES OF TOM SAWYER • Mark Twain
IVANHOE • Sir Walter Scott